MISTAKEN IN CLAYMORE RIDGE

Ben Oakes had always been involved in trouble — he'd killed men before — but now he was determined to live a new life and never to carry a weapon. But when he's wrongfully imprisoned for the murder of Todd Hankin, he's desperate to clear his name and escape the hangman's noose. Then Ben is finally released, and his search for Todd's killer leads him to Claymore Ridge, where he faces threats to his life from more than one quarter . . .

BILL WILLIAMS

MISTAKEN IN CLAYMORE RIDGE

Complete and Unabridged

LINFORD
Leicester

First published in Great Britain in 2008 by
Robert Hale Limited
London

First Linford Edition
published 2009
by arrangement with
Robert Hale Limited
London

The moral right of the author has been asserted

British Library CIP Data

Williams, Bill, *1940 –*
Mistaken in Claymore Ridge
- - (Linford western library)
1. Western stories.
2. Large type books.
I. Title II. Series
823.9′2–dc22

ISBN 978–1–84782–663–3

Published by
F. A. Thorpe (Publishing)
Anstey, Leicestershire

Set by Words & Graphics Ltd.
Anstey, Leicestershire
Printed and bound in Great Britain by
T. J. International Ltd., Padstow, Cornwall

This book is printed on acid-free paper

This book is dedicated to the late John Moorcroft and his hometown of Bootle on Merseyside. John was a fine artist and a prolific writer of poetry, mostly humorous, whose friendly and caring nature endeared him to so many people.

1

Ben Oakes grimaced when he saw the dried blood on his hands. It was Todd's blood and they said he'd killed him. But Todd Hankin had been his buddy, even though he was the son of Milton Hankin, the owner of the biggest ranch in this part of Arizona, and he was just a lowly hired hand. He looked around the cell, but there was no water bowl so that he could wash away the blood. Marshal Parrin had said he would be back later and settle him in, whatever that meant. It wasn't the first time that he'd been behind bars, but not in a cell this small. At least the blanket covering the small iron bed was clean. Why hadn't they believed him when he told them he'd found Todd by the barn and seen his killer ride off? Maybe it was because he couldn't give a description of the man! Now he was regretting not going after the killer instead of attending to Todd, but he'd just acted on instinct. Milton Hankin had looked at him with pure hate in his eyes and Todd's sister Madeline had been filled with disbelief and in a state of shock. She was only eighteen years old and her sweet face had never known tragedy until today.

Ben Oakes was just over six feet tall. His shoulders were broad and hips slim. He had let his brown hair grow long and his grey eyes could be cold and threatening, except when he was smiling. He was a man's man who was loved by womenfolk. Anyone would want him on their side in a tight situation, but he was not someone to make an enemy of.

Ben had a nagging feeling that he might actually be to blame for Todd's death. He'd lied when he'd claimed that Todd was dead when he reached him. Todd had tried to tell him something as the life ebbed from his body. None of the words made any sense, except the last one he spoke, which was Claymore. Claymore was the name of one of the biggest towns in the state of Arizona. The town's official name was Claymore Ridge which was the name of the original town that was built near a ridge some ten miles south of the existing town. Todd Hankin hadn't had an enemy in the world, but Ben could think of many who might think they had a score to settle with Ben Oakes. So, maybe the man had come looking for Ben and Todd had tried to protect him in some way, because Todd knew about Ben's past.

Ben had been experiencing some strange memory lapses and severe pains at the back of his head for many months. Todd had told him that Ben had met up with someone from his past in a saloon when they visited Claymore after they'd picked up some breeding stock. Ben had given the man a beating and had told Todd that the man was Toby Brogan, and he'd killed his brother, Ike during a shootout in Jolin

3

County. Ike had been pushing Ben into going for his gun and had just been looking for trouble.

When Ben had left the saloon on his own sometime after his fight with Toby Brogan, he had been attacked from behind and suffered a massive blow to the back of his head. Todd had brought Ben back to the Hankin ranch after he'd recovered sufficiently to travel, but Ben couldn't remember brawling with Toby Brogan, or ever being in Claymore Ridge. It seemed likely that Toby Brogan must have been Ben's attacker. Todd had remembered Ben taking Brogan's gun off him and handing it to the barman, otherwise Brogan might have shot him later. Todd had suggested that Brogan probably thought he'd left Ben for dead and left town.

Ben's thoughts were disturbed by the arrival of the marshal and his deputy, Curly Godden. Marshal Will Parrin was thirty-two years old, with broad shoulders and a barrel chest. He had powerful arms, mainly on account that he'd been a blacksmith before becoming a lawman. He was medium height, with brown hair, and looks that made him popular with the ladies. Some of the Tremaine Creek council were against his appointment because his right hand had been severed by the leader of a gang that had terrorized the town a few years earlier. Will Parrin had been his pa's deputy at the time and he ended up killing the man who'd maimed him. He'd learned to use his left hand and could outdraw most men with the Smith & Wesson pistol that had belonged to his pa and was housed in a custom-made left-handed holster.

The marshal kept his pistol trained on Ben while his deputy opened the cell and carried in the small bowl of water and then a plate of beans and a mug of hot coffee. After the cell door had been slammed shut, Marshal Parrin addressed Ben.

'Why don't you make it easier for everyone, Oakes, and confess? I don't care much for the Hankins because they wield too much power. It just isn't right that folks should be as wealthy as they are, but the family shouldn't have to suffer more than necessary. You can spare them the ordeal of a trial if you own up. You're going to hang, come what may, so you can get it over with quickly and you won't prolong their agony, or your own for that matter.'

'And you'll save the marshal a heap of paperwork,' added the deputy, with a grin that soon disappeared when the marshal glowered at him. Deputy Godden was tall and gangly. His face was boyish and when he grinned, which was often, he never seemed self-conscious about his buck teeth. Ben was thinking that he'd never seen a more unlikely lawman than Curly Godden.

Ben didn't take long to dismiss the marshal's suggestion and said, 'I'll take my chances with a jury, Marshal. Perhaps they'll believe me and remember that there are no witnesses. Billy Cobb was in the stables behind the

6

house and never said he saw me do it. He just didn't see Todd's killer ride off like I did.'

'The fact is it doesn't matter whether you did it or not. No jury in this town is going to do anything to rile Milton Hankin. Now, we know that's wrong, but that's the way it is.'

Ben was thinking maybe he should follow the marshal's advice. Why hadn't anyone else seen the rider, especially Billy who had heard the shots? He knew that Billy didn't like him too much, but he was only a young kid and he didn't seem the sort to use the opportunity to land Ben in this sort of trouble. Not unless Billy knew who the real killer was.

Marshal Parrin gave a sigh when he realized that Ben wasn't going to make life easy for the Hankins. 'Maybe you'll feel different in the morning. I've got nothing against you, Oakes. You might be as innocent as a Sunday school teacher, but that don't matter none. It's really a question of how you want to die. You might want to dwell on the thought that if you go to trial then it might take weeks for it to be set up. Now if some folks get restless and decide to do a spot of lynching then me and Curly won't be able to stop them. I've seen a man tortured by a mob and it wasn't pretty and he took a heck of a time before he drew his last breath. I'm no sensitive flower, but it was a long time before I stopped hearing his screams inside my head. Now if you plead guilty, then you have my word that you'll die quickly and with dignity.'

'The marshal always makes sure that his hangings are humane,' said Curly. 'I can vouch for that. I remember the hanging before last. It was old Joe Maitland who shot his wife dead because she burnt his dinner after he'd come home late from the saloon. Well, Joe had the fattest neck you've ever seen and he was left gasping as he dangled from the rope until the marshal drew his pistol and shot him clean between the eyes. Old Joe just gave a twitch and his suffering was over.'

'Let's go, Curly,' said the marshal. 'I think Oakes knows the score and now it's up to him. I expect he's going to have black eyes and a throbbing nose come morning.'

Ben felt the bridge of his nose that had been broken when he was attacked by some of the cowboys who'd returned from the roundup and seen him next to Todd and holding a pistol. He watched the lawmen disappear into the front office and close the linking door behind them and then he lay on the bed, wondering how long he would be here. Ben's plans for the new life he'd craved for were now in ruins because fate had delivered him a cruel hand. But he had no intention of saving the marshal from doing his paperwork, or the town council the expense of a trial.

2

Dexter Hankin had returned home and found his sister Madeline dressed in black. He'd asked if their pa had died and she'd not made much sense with all her crying before she'd said that it was their brother Todd who they had buried. Dexter had wished that it had been his pa!

Dexter was twenty-five years old. He was almost six feet tall, slim built, had brown hair and grey eyes. The broad nose, the result of a boyhood accident, gave him a rugged look and a false impression, because he had never been in a brawl, or even a schoolboy fight. He relied on smooth talking to get himself out of trouble, although it never worked with his pa. He and Todd had always been different, and not exactly close. He remembered seeing his brother head upstairs with one of the girls from the Muncaster Saloon in the local town of Tremaine Creek. Ben Oakes had been with them then, and now folks were accusing him of murder, even though he didn't carry a gun. Dexter recalled the time he and Todd persuaded Ben to join in when they were out target shooting. He was awesome with a pistol and put the brothers to shame. The following day Todd had told Dexter some of the things that Ben had confided in him about his past which explained why his shooting had been so impressive.

Dexter didn't really blame his pa for lashing out at him and not sparing his feelings when he ranted at him for not being present at his own brother's funeral. Dexter had some serious thinking to do because his pa had made it clear that he wouldn't be financing any more of his trips away. Dexter had hoped his pa would realize that just because Todd had gone it didn't mean that he could

11

suddenly take to ranching. He would have to try and keep in his pa's good books until he decided what to do. Maybe if he stayed at home he could meet and marry a rich rancher's daughter and then he wouldn't have to rely upon his pa's money any more. Meg Lincoln's pa was rich enough for Dexter's purposes. She was reasonably attractive with a wholesome body, but he would find it hard getting used to the way she snorted when she laughed. The other problem was that she was too nice and fond of reading her Bible. He liked his women to be feisty, even a bit wild. If he did end up marrying her then he would just have to be a dutiful husband and keep her pregnant. He could always arrange to do lots of travelling away on business. He didn't know what business it would be, except he would make sure that it would be one that would take him to where the best saloon girls were.

★ ★ ★

Dexter had made an excuse for not joining Madeline when she went to pay another visit to the cemetery to lay fresh flowers on Todd's grave and, after breakfast, he went to his pa's oak-panelled study. Milton gave Dexter a cursory glance and then continued his book-keeping as Dexter stood in front of the large desk like a timid employee. He waited for his pa to acknowledge his presence, but he didn't.

Milton Hankin was shorter than his sons. He was still lean, despite his rich living, and even before the recent tragedy his face had usually been set in a serious expression. Now the dark eyes had lost their threatening look and were dead. The brown hair, with strands of grey, was no longer well groomed and he hadn't changed his clothes since the funeral.

'Pa, is there anything I can do to help?' Dexter asked timidly, sounding more like a nervous schoolboy than a grown man.

'Help, what sort of help do you have in mind?' Milton replied, in a mocking voice. 'Perhaps you want to organize a memorial party for all the neighbours. Erect a marquee and order in some fine wines; make a fancy speech and lie about how you loved your brother. Is that what you mean by help?'

'I have feelings as well, Pa, and I'm missing Todd as much as you and Madeline.'

'Sure you are,' Milton said sarcastically. 'If you really want to help then you can go and select a length of rope, take some of the men into town and drag your brother's killer out of his cell and hang him from the nearest tree.'

'Pa, times have changed. Do you want me to hang as well for lynching Ben Oakes? Is that what you really want?'

It was the first time he'd seen his pa cry! He didn't know what to do as the man who'd always been in control of everything sobbed into his hands.

'Is that what you really want, Pa?' Dexter repeated, sensing that his pa was vulnerable.

Milton rubbed the tears from his face with one of his large rough hands as he gathered his composure again.

'I know that if Oakes had killed you then Todd would have taken care of things. Now leave me be to get on with my work. I don't want to talk anymore. If you've nothing better to do then you might join your sister at the cemetery.'

Dexter left his pa and wondered if perhaps he should go and call on Meg Lincoln, but decided that they might think it inappropriate to go courting so soon after his brother's death. He was also thinking that maybe he should only be thinking of Meg as a last resort. Perhaps his pa would mellow once he got over his grieving after Ben Oakes was left swinging from the end of a rope.

⋆　⋆　⋆

15

Come the evening Dexter was tempted to wait until dark and go into town and have himself a saloon girl, but decided that wasn't the best way to please his pa. So, when the rest of the house was asleep he made his way to the servants' quarters that were located in an extension to the main house.

The light was visible under the housemaid's door and he had a feeling that his night was going to become bearable after all. He could have gone to the bunkhouse and played cards, but that was more Todd's style, mixing with the hired help. Maribel was no Mexican beauty and in some ways reminded him of Meg, not in looks, but in her demeanour. Like Meg she would have no experience of being with a man. He'd seen her wearing her rosary beads and was certain that she would have been brought up to be a good girl and save herself for the man she would marry. She was a sweet innocent girl, the kind who always had a certain appeal for him, although he

16

preferred women wh... pleasure a man. He n... pay for their experience, ... he'd had the pleasure of ... married woman, like Beth Hingt... wife of the Hankin foreman, D... Hington. Beth was a bit younger than her husband and had always made it obvious that she had feelings for Dexter and she'd shown them during their secret meetings. She was one passionate woman and they could have still been enjoying each other if she hadn't started talking about leaving her husband. Dexter ended it by telling her that she was just too old for him and she was hurt, really hurt. He was confident that he had put an end to her pestering.

Dexter tapped gently on the bedroom door for the second time before it was slowly opened and Maribel stood before him. The hair that he'd only ever seen pinned back lay on her shoulders and the long, white nightdress was unbuttoned. Could this olive-skinned

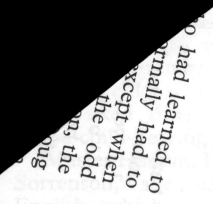

plain, nervous
d his breakfast
e wide hips that
e apron were just
e'd heard them
ips.

hought it was Mrs
d in her broken
found cute. He
wondered w.... guage she would call
out in while they were making love!

Maribel pulled her nightdress across
her body to hide her bare flesh and she
lowered her eyes.

He couldn't believe his luck. This girl
was the real thing. A sweet innocent,
religious girl, who had been taught by
her mama to control her passion and
keep herself pure. She had saved herself
for her wedding night, but he intended
to be the first. She could always lie to
her stupid husband.

'I'm feeling a bit sad about my
brother's death and I haven't got
anyone to talk to,' said Dexter in his
most sombre voice. 'My sister and pa

are too upset. I have a feeling that you are a person who cares about others and you're more than just a very beautiful woman.'

Dexter could tell that no one had ever told her she was beautiful before and while she was dwelling on it he eased past her into the room and sat on the small bed.

Maribel looked out into the corridor as if checking if anyone was watching and then stepped back into her room and closed the door.

'I'm sorry, I shouldn't be burdening you with my trouble,' he apologized. 'I guess coming here with my sorrow isn't very manly of me. I'd better go.' Dexter stood up and waited for her reaction.

'Master Hankin, it must be bad for you losing your brother. I have lost dear ones myself,' she said as her eyes filled with tears.

'You should call me Dexter if we're going to be friends and I need a friend right now.'

'Please stay and talk, if it helps you,'

19

she said, and touched his arm in a gesture of comfort. He smiled when he took her hand, sat down on the bed and guided her to sit beside him. He touched the small tear on her cheek and said, 'You really are a special sort of person and I hope you'll always stay that way.'

Dexter questioned Maribel about her family and made a string of flattering remarks about her eyes, hair and beautiful skin. He held her hand and asked if he could kiss her and he was amused when she seemed shocked as she lowered her eyes once again.

'I've wanted to kiss you, Maribel, ever since the very first time I saw you and I hoped you might feel the same way.' He didn't wait for her to reply and leaned forward, kissing her gently on the lips. She didn't resist and he kissed her again. This time it was longer and he slowly eased her back on to the bed. She gave up her half-hearted attempt to push him away when he whispered into her ear, 'You're so beautiful, beautiful.

The most beautiful woman I have ever seen.'

She returned his kisses, but her body stiffened in panic when his hand reached beneath her nightdress and rested on the soft, smooth flesh of her inner thigh. 'Don't be frightened,' he whispered, and then began exploring her body. She moaned when his fingers gently squeezed one of her nipples. He kept eye contact as he rose from the bed and stripped away his clothes. She resisted once more when he started to remove her nightdress. But her resistance ended when he told her that she was helping him forget his pain.

He made love to her in frenzy as she lay frozen in fear, but offering no resistance. His grunts turned to a final groan before he pulled away from her and began dressing as quickly as he had undressed a few minutes earlier.

'I'd better be going. I have a busy day ahead,' he said in a bored voice and then yawned.

Maribel sat up and pulled a sheet

across her breasts and watched him finish dressing. 'Maybe you could take me on a picnic when I finish my work tomorrow,' she suggested.

'I think my pa's going to keep me pretty busy, Maribel, until I head out of here and do a bit more travelling. But I'll be thinking of you.'

He left the room, not caring that he might have ruined Maribel's life just to satisfy his lust.

Dexter paused briefly outside Maribel's door and sighed before he started his walk along the corridor that led to the main house. He swirled around, startled by Mrs Sorrenson's voice as she asked him what he wanted, but being an accomplished liar he quickly recovered and replied, 'I'm planning to make an early start tomorrow morning and I just asked the Mexican girl if she'd prepare me an early breakfast.'

'What time would you like it?' Mrs Sorrenson asked, her eyes focusing on his undone shirt buttons and unbuckled belt.

'About nine o'clock, if that's not too early,' he replied.

'Your father breakfasts much earlier than that so you needn't have troubled yourself by coming up here.'

'Fine. I'll be on my way and sorry to have disturbed you both,' he said, eager to get away from the nosy old bitch.

Dexter walked on, cursing under his breath, but Mrs Sorrenson called after him.

'If ever you need anything, Master Dexter, it would be better if you came to see me. My door is always open to the needs of the family, day or night, but I expect you know that already.'

Dexter wasn't sure whether Mrs Sorrenson was offering herself to him, or perhaps it was just her way of telling him that she knew what he was up to. Mrs Sorrenson reminded him of his Aunt Phyllis with her hair tied in a bun and bosoms that seemed to rest on her large stomach. He'd lost his virginity to a previous housekeeper who hadn't been much younger than

Mrs Sorrenson, and he had blushed every time he saw her curvy body. He'd realized later that she had teased him and made sure that he saw more of her than he should have done. There had been a few occasions when she had stood close to him, and others when she had pressed her body against his while leaning over at the table. He had lost his virginity on the night of his sixteenth birthday and he'd been as embarrassed as hell afterwards. He managed to get her dismissed by planting items in her room which she was accused of stealing. Now he would have to think of a way to make sure that the interfering old busybody Mrs Sorrenson was sent packing, but first he would make sure Maribel wouldn't be around for much longer. She had been a big disappointment and he wouldn't be seeking the use of her body again. It might have been different if she'd tried to fight him off by putting up some resistance and showing some emotion. She hadn't even scratched him!

3

Dexter was late joining his pa for breakfast and he received a knowing look from Mrs Sorrenson and a shy smile from Maribel. Dexter took one sip of his coffee and snapped at Maribel for serving it to him cold. She tried to explain that it was freshly made, but Dexter cut her short, 'Don't argue with me, missy. Fetch me some fresh coffee.'

Maribel hurried away with the steaming hot coffee pot and managed to hold back her tears until she reached the kitchen. She had just experienced the real Dexter Hankin who had dashed her hopes that they might have a special relationship. Her mama had warned her about men like Dexter Hankin and now she was regretting not heeding her advice.

As Dexter was finishing his breakfast he told his pa that he was intending to ride out and give a hand with the herd.

'Make sure you help the boys and not hinder them,' said Milton, as he rose from the table and left the room, while shaking his head as a sign of annoyance with his son.

★ ★ ★

Dexter had changed into dark clothes and selected a black Stetson from his large selection before heading for the stables behind the magnificent ranch house. His arrival at the stables startled Billy Cobb who was grooming Milton Hankin's sorrel.

'Sorry, Master Hankin,' Billy apologized. 'I ain't usually so jumpy, but I suppose it's because of what happened.'

Billy was just seventeen years old, slightly built and some would say good-looking, but for his cross eyes which usually meant that he was looking down or away when in conversation. He'd let his black hair grow long so that it hung over one eye in the form of a natural patch, but he often forgot and flicked it away from his face.

'Would you like me to saddle the stallion, sir? He's already been groomed and I think he's raring to go. He's a fine horse.'

'No, saddle up Speckly. I think he might need the exercise more. My horse must still be tired from the long ride we had getting here, so he's earned a rest.'

Billy looked uncomfortable. 'Mister Hankin said that no one was to ride your brother's horse.'

'I don't think he had me in mind when he said that. I'll probably ride him from now on. He's the best horse we've ever had and he's too lively for my pa or my sister to ride so I guess he's mine now. But you can use my saddle. That one of Todd's is all right, but I prefer my custom built one Pa bought me for my special birthday.'

Billy had no intention of arguing with Dexter and he had soon saddled up the distinctive grey that had identical black streaks on its flanks. He wondered how many months, or even years of his wages it would have needed to pay for Dexter's saddle with its fancy patterns carved into the leather and silver buckles.

Dexter climbed up onto the grey and when it objected to him on its back he dug his spurs into its flesh. He'd ridden the animal many times before without any problems and wondered if it had sensed something had happened to its master. But he soon got the animal under control and was heading out of the stable when he pulled on the reins and then turned and addressed Billy. 'Cobb, are you absolutely certain that you never saw anyone here on the day my brother was killed?'

Billy looked anxious before he replied, 'It was like I told the marshal. I heard the shots and thought Master Todd was practising, then when I went to get some grub just after that I saw Ben Oakes with a gun in his hand. Then the cowhands came riding in and they saw him as well.'

'What about before the shooting. Did you see anyone else? Perhaps one of the cowboys who'd come back early from the roundup? Was there anyone, even family, or people you might not suspect?'

'Only,' Billy faltered for a moment and then continued, 'only the Mexican girl who had been taking some washing off the line, but that was some time before the shooting, I think.'

'Good,' said Dexter, and dug his spurs into the horse's flesh to urge it forward and he didn't hear Billy say, 'I'll be carrying this from now on in case there's more trouble.' Billy had tapped the second-hand Colt .44 that he'd bought from the general store in Tremaine Creek the day before Todd was killed. He'd only fired it twice, but he planned to do some practising later. He'd do it to make sure that he would be able to defend Miss Madeline if he had to, but mainly because he had a feeling he might need to protect himself.

Dexter pushed the grey hard and he was soon on the high ground above the small valley where Milton Hankin had built their house. Dexter looked down and marvelled at his birthplace. On all his travels he'd never seen a finer looking house. The Hankin spread was just about the biggest in this corner of Arizona mainly due to the land that his mother, Elizabeth, inherited when her pa, Thomas Fairbrass, had died. The combination of Hankin and Fairbrass land had allowed Milton to expand even further by buying up more land from some smaller ranch owners who had given up trying to compete with him at the cattle markets. Milton had dropped a few hints that he would welcome the idea of a merger with the Lincoln ranch if ever Dexter married Herbert Lincoln's only daughter, Meg. If Dexter married Meg it would be to get his hands on the Lincolns' wealth and not to please his pa. Everyone knew that Todd had always been the favourite and once their mother had died his pa just handed Dexter money whenever he needed it. It was almost as though he didn't want to set eyes on him. If he and Todd had not looked so alike he might have thought maybe Milton Hankin wasn't his real pa. He'd seen photographs of his ma when she was young and she had been a fine-looking woman. Who could have blamed her for going astray if Milton had neglected her by spending too much time building up his ranching empire! There would have been no shortage of men amongst the hired help willing to pay her attention and give her the compliments and smooth talking that all women craved for.

Dexter was in no doubt that his pa's only interest in him now was that he would provide the means for keeping the Hankin name alive. Milton Hankin had been an only child, like his pa before him, and now with Todd gone it would fall to Dexter to father a son. Dexter already had at least one son who was born to a saloon girl in a small town in northern Arizona. Dexter had seen the baby boy just the once and given the mother some money. He would never tell his pa about the boy because Milton's desire for the continuation of the Hankin name would not extend to welcoming a little bastard into his house. Nor would he want his son to marry a whore.

4

Ewen Macey was branding the last calf when he saw Dexter Hankin approach. Dexter was a stuck-up son of a bitch, except when he wanted something. Well, Macey had a plan that might just appeal to Mister high and mighty Dexter Hankin.

Macey had worked on the Hankin Ranch since he was a boy of fifteen, nearly seven years ago. Milton Hankin was a hard task master, but Macey had never been afraid of hard work and he'd enjoyed the life, until the arrival of Ben Oakes. Oakes was a complete stranger and yet the whole of the Hankin family seemed to think he was something special, even Madeline. He'd watched Madeline grow from a gawky-looking girl with those silly pigtails, into a woman that any man would lust over given a chance. Well,

Ewen always thought that he had a chance because Madeline liked him, liked him a lot.

Ewen Macey was a mite less than six feet tall, with brown hair and brown eyes that usually had a twinkle in them, except when he was brooding over something. Macey knew that he could take his pick from the girls he'd grown up with. Even some married women had come on strong with him. Beth Hington, the foreman's wife, was forever pestering him to teach her to ride. She'd said that her husband didn't have the patience, skill, or know how to treat a woman with understanding. She was sure that Ewen wasn't like that. Ewen had escorted Madeline to the special Easter Dance in the town for the past two years, but this year she had made some excuse about spraining her ankle, but he knew it was a lie. Madeline was sweet on Ben Oakes and that was why she had given him the cold shoulder.

Macey wouldn't be missing Todd and

it looked as though Oakes wouldn't be around to spoil his future plans for him and Madeline. So, things might work out just fine. Some of the cowhands believed that Oakes was innocent, but what did it matter, because Milton Hankin didn't. Hankin had grown up in times when men took care of things themselves and didn't rely upon the law to give a man the punishment he deserved. Macey could see that there was a way to make sure that Oakes was out of the way for good and at the same time please Milton Hankin. The only problem was that he had to make sure that Hankin knew that he'd taken care of Oakes without Madeline finding out.

Macey greeted Dexter and then asked, 'What brings you amongst us working folk?'

Dexter slipped down from the grey and when he told him that he'd ridden out to give a hand, Macey struggled to stop himself from smirking. Come the day that Dexter gave a hand it would be the first time, because hard work and Dexter just didn't mix. Dexter believed in enjoying himself and wouldn't let work get in the way of that. Macey suspected that old man Hankin actually approved of what his fun-loving son did with his life. Perhaps he could see him doing the things he'd never been able to do when he was young. Sure, he gave Dexter a hard time for all his pleasure seeking, but did he actually disapprove? It might be different in the future with Todd gone, but only time would tell. Macey was hoping that if his plan worked out then he would end up with Oakes's old job and work near the ranch house. That way he could comfort Madeline over the loss of her brother and things would soon be back the way they were before golden boy, Ben Oakes, came in from nowhere and messed things up.

'We were all sorry to hear about your brother,' said Macey, as he took the reins of Dexter's horse and tied them to the fence that formed the branding pen.

Dexter didn't acknowledge the gesture of sympathy, except for a weak smile and said, 'It looks as though I've arrived too late to help you with the branding. Perhaps next time I'll ride out a bit earlier.'

'I expect things are a bit sad around the place,' Macey suggested while taking off his Stetson and wiping away the sweat from his forehead before replacing the hat.

'Gloomy would be a better word, but I expect things will get better when Oakes's trial is over.'

'So the sly shooter hasn't owned up to save your family more heartache in court,' said Macey, his tone showing his disgust.

'Marshal Parrin rode by yesterday and told Pa that Oakes is still claiming his innocence, despite there being no one who can back up his story.'

'Still, justice will be done once he goes on trial. How does your pa feel about all this? I expect you must have all been shocked after the way the family welcomed Oakes as though he was someone special.'

'Pa hates the man and to be honest, I'm surprised he hasn't taken the law into his own hands. He doesn't trust the courts and because no one actually saw Oakes pull the trigger he thinks that the jury will let him off. Oakes will claim that he had no motive for killing Todd and if he did, why would he risk doing it so close to the house.'

'You really think your pa might consider doing something before the trial starts?' Macey asked.

Dexter looked worried and replied, 'I honestly don't know. I suppose he would have done it by now, if he was going to, but who knows what will happen when the trial gets closer? Pa is so convinced that Oakes is guilty I don't think he could face the idea of him getting away with it. Pa and my brother were very close, you know that. I just don't think he could live with himself if Todd's killer didn't pay with his own life.'

Macey decided that this was the opportunity he'd been waiting for, but he paused while he considered what to say.

'Your pa is a very experienced man and a law-abiding one, but I share his concerns about justice not always being delivered. I'm glad you came by because I can tell you that me and some of the boys are planning to make sure that Oakes gets what he deserves.' Macey reached for the canteen of water tied to the fence and offered it to Dexter who declined with a shake of his head. Macey took a long gulp of water waiting for Dexter to respond to his suggestion.

'You mean a lynch mob, don't you?' asked Dexter, who was taken aback by the suggestion.

'It may not be a lynching, more a grilling because we favour burning him alive in his cell. Hanging is too good for his sort,' replied Macey without a trace of emotion and added, 'We'll be wearing masks and we'll threaten to shoot any do-gooder that tries to put the fire out. It's planned for tomorrow night because I heard that Marshal Parrin will be out of town. You can tell your pa that his concerns will be over. Your family have always been good to me and this will be my way of repaying you, but I wouldn't want Madeline finding out about this because she might not understand. Your sister's too trusting of people, but I guess that's the way she's been brought up.'

Dexter liked the idea because it would mean that his pa would get off his back, but he wasn't prepared to put his own neck on the line. When Macey suggested that maybe he'd like to ride with them, Dexter gave a heavy sigh and pondered as though he was considering the offer.

Macey had another suggestion. 'It might be fitting for you to throw the torch to start the fire going. I know I'd want to if it was my brother's killer in there. We'd just tag along to give you our support. We wouldn't want to steal your glory.'

'I'd really like to, Ewen, because like you said, Oakes took us all in, but there are some things I need to consider and I don't mean for myself. What you are planning to do is brave, but also very risky. If I joined you and things went wrong then my pa would end up losing another son and I don't think I should risk that, do you?'

Macey had got the answer he'd expected, but said he understood. He understood all right. He could read Dexter Hankin like a book. The smarmy son of a bitch had a yeller streak running down his back.

When Dexter asked if the other men involved could be trusted, Macey just smiled and said, 'That won't be a problem because I've just decided to do this on my own. Maybe it's best not to involve anyone else in case they start blabbing. There's always someone with a loose tongue after liquor. Marshal Parrin will be as mad as hell when he finds out and he'll want to catch whoever did it. You're right about it being risky, but I think I can manage to burn the marshal's office down on my own.'

'You really do intend to burn Oakes alive?' asked Dexter, while trying not to show his squeamishness.

'I couldn't manage a lynching on my own. But I wouldn't want to do anything you didn't agree with. I'm doing this for your family, not for myself. Do you have a problem with me burning him in his cell?'

'No,' replied Dexter quickly and then added, 'Oakes deserves all he gets.'

'Good, as long as it's clear that I have the support of the Hankin family.'

'You have,' said Dexter in another show of bravado. He was eager to end this gruesome conversation. He wished Macey luck and then said he was heading back to tell his pa the news. He was sure that his pa would reward Macey's loyalty in some way.

Macey watched Dexter gallop away,

shook his head and smiled. Things couldn't have worked out better. He could look forward to marrying Madeline and maybe owning the fine horse he'd just seen being whipped by Dexter Hankin as he rode off.

5

Ben hadn't expected anyone to visit him, except perhaps a lynch mob. But he was in for a surprise when the deputy announced that someone from the Hankin ranch wanted to see him. Ben couldn't think who it might be, but whoever it was it had caused the deputy some amusement because he was grinning. Curly Godden was the tallest and probably the thinnest man in town.

Ben rose from the bed ready to greet Madeline Hankin as she approached his cell. He noted the reddened eyes indicating that she hadn't done with weeping yet. Her straight blonde hair was tied up with a ribbon and she looked older and more severe looking. Maybe it was being dressed all in black, and wearing a shawl that made her look so different to the image he'd been picturing while lying on his bed.

'I didn't kill, Todd, Madeline. I swear to you that I didn't,' Ben blurted out before Madeline even spoke.

'I know, that's why I'm here, Ben.'

'How do you know?' he asked, hoping that she had some news for him that would prove that he wasn't lying. 'Have you found out something?' he asked, without waiting for her to reply to his first question.

'No, I just know that you couldn't do such a thing. Daddy thinks you killed Todd, but he doesn't know you like I do and he's so stricken with grief that he just isn't thinking straight.'

Ben wondered if she would feel the same way if she knew about his past. The truth was that Madeline didn't know the real Ben Oakes, the one whose ways he had tried to put behind him. He'd done things that no man would be proud of. He'd taken a human life more than once when his pride had stopped him from just walking away. There was only one occasion when he had no regrets and that was when he'd killed for the first time.

Ben sensed her discomfort and asked her why she'd really come to see him and said that he didn't want to cause her any upset.

'I came to warn you, Ben. You're in danger, because there's going to be some sort of raid on the jail while Marshal Parrin is away. It's going to happen tonight! I only heard odd bits. He's planning to . . . ' Madeline couldn't finish her words and her eyes filled with tears.

'He's aiming to lynch me. That's what you've come to warn me about,' he said, then regretted being so blunt. But he was shocked when she told him that a man on his own was going to burn down his cell with him inside it.

'Perhaps if we told Deputy Godden he could move you somewhere, at least until the marshal gets back,' Madeline suggested, her voice full of anguish. It pained him to see her suffering.

'I'd only be safe until the next time

and not even Marshal Parrin can stop anyone if they're determined enough. There's only one way out of this for me, Madeline. I need to escape and find the man who shot Todd and you can help me if you really believe I'm innocent.'

'But how?' she asked, unable to see what she could do.

After Ben had finished telling her about his plan, she just said, 'But what if Deputy Godden is too smart to fall for it?'

Ben smiled. 'I don't think we need worry on that score. This is my only chance, Madeline. If it works then you must say that you came to tell me that you hoped I would rot in hell. You can say I slapped you through the bars of the cell and threatened to get some of my friends to kill your pa if you didn't fetch me the cell keys. Tell them anything you want about me if it helps keep you out of trouble. And, Madeline' — he paused and then added — 'thanks for this and for believing me. I promise you that I'll do everything I can to find Todd's killer.'

'Ben, there's something I've got to ask you.'

'Don't look so worried. What is it?'

'I saw you and Todd arguing by the corral the day before he was killed. You looked really upset and angry about something.'

Ben rubbed the back of his head as he replied, 'It was all a bit stupid and my fault, but we laughed about it later. Todd mentioned something that happened four months ago and I said I couldn't remember it. He said I must be able to remember and I must be stupid if I couldn't. It got a bit heated for awhile, and then, as I said, we laughed about it. It was nothing really.'

'Where will you go?' she asked, satisfied with his explanation, but wondering if they'd argued over a girl.

'I'll head for Claymore Ridge because I'm certain that Todd's killer doesn't come from around here. He might be a drifter, but I'm guessing he might just end up in a town the size of Claymore.'

Ben didn't like lying to her about the real reason he was going to Claymore because that was the last word that Todd had spoken before he died.

'But how will you recognize him. You told the marshal that you didn't really get a good look at him.'

'It isn't going to be easy, Madeline, but it's the only chance I've got to clear my name and avoid a noose around my neck.'

'You'll need money,' she said, and undid the small bag she was carrying and handed him a wad of dollar bills and explained, 'I was meant to pay this into the bank for Daddy.'

Ben took the money from her knowing that it would be a great help when he got to Claymore. He could buy new clothes, visit the saloon or barber and other places where he could ask questions that might help him find the killer. The killer had to be linked to Claymore Ridge, but how, was a question that Ben had been pondering. Madeline told him that Dexter was home and when he asked her if Dexter believed Ben had killed their brother she just said that Dexter would believe anything their daddy did.

'I won't forget this, Madeline,' he said, and then told her to lie on the floor and act as though she had fainted. As soon as she was in position he shouted, 'Help, Deputy, get some help in here. Something has happened to Miss Hankin!'

Deputy Godden rushed in, looking confused and flustered. Then he saw Madeline lying on the floor near Ben's cell. 'Jesus, what have you done to her?' he roared at Ben.

'How could I do anything from behind these bars, you dumb ass. She just fainted. Get Doc Baxter and make it quick. She doesn't look too good.'

'What if the doc isn't there, or he's drunk?' the deputy asked.

'Then get someone else. Get Mrs Coleman from the store, she'll know what to do.'

Deputy Godden was staring down at

Madeline as though willing her to show some signs of life.

'Move,' Ben roared, and the deputy finally hurried away.

Within seconds of hearing the office door close, Ben told Madeline to get up and go and look for the keys, hoping that the deputy hadn't grabbed them on his way out. He heaved a sigh of relief when Madeline returned with the large bunch of keys and set about trying to open the cell.

'Just take it slowly, Madeline,' Ben said calmly, while he watched her fumble in panic as she tried to discover the right key. She must have been close to trying the last key when he heard the lock click. He pushed open the heavy cell door then rushed to the main office and began searching the drawers of the marshal's desk. He found a pistol and gunbelt and pocketed a handful of shells for the Winchester rifle that was on the desk.

Madeline had followed Ben into the office and he reminded her again, 'Just tell them what I told you, Madeline. But you mustn't tell anyone that I'm heading for Claymore because they'll hunt me down and I'll end up back in the cell and your help will have been for nothing.'

She watched him hurry out into the street. 'Be careful,' she said, even though she knew that he couldn't hear her.

Deputy Godden was flustered and confused once again when he returned and found Madeline sitting in a chair in the main office area.

'That son of a bitch just rode off on my horse and he's stolen the Winchester I was cleaning. Marshal Parrin will have my balls for this.' The deputy blushed with embarrassment, apologized for his language and then asked Madeline if she was feeling better. Before she answered, Doc Baxter arrived carrying his small bag. He wasn't drunk and gave her a kindly smile and asked the same question as the deputy.

Doc Baxter was sixty-two years old and his red jovial face had not suffered from witnessing so many horrors and tragedy in his work as a medical man, or from the excesses of the alcohol to which he frequently subjected his small framed body.

She told him that she was fine and just hadn't been eating well these last few days.

Deputy Godden shook his head and said. 'I don't understand how Oakes got the keys because they were hanging up in the office. He couldn't have reached them from his cell unless he's a magician as well as a killer.'

Madeline was thinking that the deputy wasn't as dumb as Ben had thought, but it didn't matter because she didn't intend to lie about what had happened.

'I gave him the keys and I didn't faint,' Madeline admitted.

'You mean you helped him escape?' Deputy Godden blurted out in disbelief. 'You helped your own brother's killer escape? He must have threatened you in some way. Is that why you did it?'

'He didn't threaten me,' Madeline shouted, as her eyes swelled with tears. 'He's not like that and he didn't kill my brother. Ben Oakes is a good, kind and honest man.'

'Well you're the only one that believes that, Madeline,' said Doc Baxter who had already decided that the silly girl was probably besotted with Oakes and he must have spun her a yarn. She wasn't the first and wouldn't be the last woman to believe a man despite all the evidence that he was a no-good or perhaps even worse in the case of Ben Oakes.

'How could you do that?' asked Deputy Godden who was still baffled by what had happened and worried what Marshal Parrin would have to say about him being fooled by Madeline's play-acting.

'Someone was planning to burn his cell down.'

'Oakes told you that and you believed him?' asked Deputy Godden.

'It was me who told Ben because I heard someone at our ranch talking about it.'

'Who was it, Madeline?' the doc asked in a gentle manner. 'Who wanted to do such a horrible thing? No man deserves to die like that.'

'I don't know, Dr Baxter, and that's the truth. I only know that it was one man on his own, but I don't know his name and I won't tell who I heard talking about it. I can't do that and no one can make me tell.'

'I'm going to have to lock you up, Miss Hankin,' said Deputy Godden showing a rare glimpse of his serious side. 'Marshal Parrin will be back in a couple of days and he'll decide what to do. I'll borrow a horse and go and tell your folks what's happened. I expect they'll want to come and visit you and maybe bring you some clothes and things.' Madeline suddenly realized the seriousness of what she'd done and she looked anxious. It had seemed the right thing to do, but now she knew why Ben had told her to lie about helping him.

'I'm sorry for causing so much trouble, but I'm not sorry that I helped Ben,' Madeline said in a quiet and tired voice.

'Now hold on, Deputy,' said Doc Baxter in a challenging tone. 'There's no need to do that. Let the girl go home until Marshal Parrin gets back. You're forgetting this young lady has been through hell these past days since her brother was killed. She's probably been confused and acting out of character. No one is going to want to see her punished for what she did.'

Deputy Godden pondered what the doc had said and then declared, 'I suppose it makes sense to let her go home, but Oakes hasn't helped his case by escaping. Now everyone will say that it proves he's as guilty as sin and sweet talked Miss Hankin into helping him.'

Doc Baxter didn't want the deputy to have second thoughts and he put his arm around Madeline and said, 'Come on, Madeline, I'll take you home.' The doc then had some comforting words for Deputy Godden. 'I think you've made a wise decision, Deputy, and so will Marshal Parrin when he gets back. Milton Hankin is not a man to upset if the marshal wants to get re-elected again for another term. You might just have kept you and the marshal from looking for another job.'

*   *   *

Milton Hankin had never raised his voice against the daughter he worshipped, but he struggled to control his temper after Doc Baxter had left after delivering her home.

'I'm sorry, Daddy. I know it was wrong, but I saw more of Ben and Todd together than anyone else. I just know he couldn't have done it. And I didn't want to lose another brother if Dexter had killed Ben and then faced a hanging.' Dexter was standing next to his sister and was surprised by what she had said, but didn't comment.

'I'm disappointed in you, Madeline, but I'm not forgetting that we were all taken in by Ben Oakes. The fact is we knew nothing about him.'

Madeline remained silent and her daddy continued, 'Why did you think Dexter would have been involved in killing Oakes?'

'I overheard you and Dexter talking about the marshal's office being burned down.'

'But that had nothing to do with Dexter. He was just passing on something he'd heard the men talking about. If you hadn't have been sneaking around then none of this would have happened, and Oakes would still be locked up.'

Madeline's eyes filled with tears and she shouted back, 'And he'd've been dead come tomorrow. I hope he keeps riding when he gets to Claymore Ridge.' Madeline rushed from the room with tears streaming down her face.

Dexter had been looking on, slightly embarrassed by the exchange between his sister and his pa and offered to go after her.

'Leave her be,' Milton ordered. 'We have important business to discuss. Close that door. We don't want Madeline or anyone else hearing what I've got to say.'

Dexter closed the door and sat in the soft leather chair in front of the desk and watched his pa's thoughtful expression, waiting to hear what the important business was.

'Do you think he really has gone to Claymore, like Madeline said, or is she trying to mislead us?' Dexter asked, doing his best to sound interested, when he wasn't.

'Your sister isn't that devious. Oakes might have lied to her about Claymore to put everyone off from following him if he knew that Claymore was outside Marshal Parrin's jurisdiction.'

'So what can we do, Pa?'

'I think there's a good chance he

might be heading for Claymore. He might have told Madeline not to tell anyone and she just blurted it out. So, I want you and Macey to head for Claymore as quick as you can. He can't have more than a couple of hours' start and you might catch up with him even before he gets there, or wherever he's heading for.'

'What do you want us to do, if we catch up with him, Pa?'

Milton Hankin shook his head in despair.

'I want you to do what Ewen Macey planned to do tonight and that's kill the bastard. I want you to avenge your brother's death.'

Dexter Hankin was cursing his luck for not avoiding all this aggravation. He just wasn't cut out for this sort of thing, but he didn't intend to argue with his father, not over this. Maybe he could turn it to his advantage without putting himself in too much danger.

'I'm ready to do what you want, Pa, except that I'd rather go after him alone. This is a family thing and I'm feeling a bit guilty for not taking the lead on this. I want to do it for Todd and to prove to you that there's more to me than just being a fun lover. There's a serious and responsible side to me that you just haven't seen.'

Milton Hankin paused and stared at his son before saying, 'All right, but you'd better not be bullshitting me, Dexter. I'm going to give you even more of an incentive to take care of Oakes and it will help you keep your resolve.'

Dexter tried to keep his composure as he waited to hear what his pa had in mind.

'If you don't find Oakes and kill him, or find that he's already dead, then don't ever come back here because, son or no son, I'll have you run off Hankin land. Now go and prove to me that you're the man I always hoped you'd be.'

Dexter was wishing his pa an early grave, but just said, 'I won't let you down, Pa, and that's a promise.'

Milton Hankin watched Dexter leave the room. He didn't expect to ever see him again.

Dexter headed straight for his room and packed some clothes before he stopped by the kitchen and ordered some food for his long journey. When Maribel handed him the food she gave him a look that left him wondering if she might have added some poison to it. He was glad that he didn't see Madeline before he left the house because he would have ended up lying to her.

Dexter urged Speckly into a gallop as he left the Hankin ranch, but he was in no hurry to catch up with Oakes and would soon be easing the animal back into a slow trot once he was out of view. He had considered paying Ewen Macey to go after Oakes while he lay low somewhere, but he knew that he couldn't trust Macey to keep any deal a secret. He was hoping that when he found out where Oakes was he would discover that he was already dead.

6

Ben had ridden for nearly two hours before he stopped close to the hills north of Tremaine Creek. Deputy Godden's black gelding had been tied to the hitch rail outside the marshal's office and Ben had heard the deputy roar after him as it galloped down Main Street. He had wondered if the deputy might use Madeline's horse to chase after him, but he didn't. He had headed for the hills intending to lie low for a few hours before he headed back to the trail that would lead to Claymore Ridge. He didn't expect the law to come after him, at least not until Marshal Parrin returned, but there was a good chance that the lynching party might. He just hoped that his pursuers would have no reason to head for Claymore.

Ben paused as he started to strip the

saddle from the tallest horse he'd ever ridden, and he hoped it would carry him to safety. If he got caught he would be in even bigger trouble now that he had escaped. He smiled at the thought that he could be in bigger trouble. Trouble didn't get any bigger than facing a hanging. He started to fasten the straps he'd just loosened intending to leave the trail and just ride on and perhaps settle in another state. Then he remembered his promise to Madeline and quickly unsaddled the horse. He was going to rest up and then head for Claymore Ridge.

Ben had led the horse to a watering-hole and filled up his canteen before heading back to his hiding place and settling down for some sleep. His ears had pricked a few times and he peered between the rocks to see if he could spot any riders coming his way, but he figured it was just his imagination playing tricks. His plan to have a short rest didn't happen when he drifted into a deep sleep, the first he'd had since being arrested.

* ★ ★

When first light came it took him a while to gather his thoughts as he looked around wondering if he was dreaming when he saw the clear blue sky and breathed in the clean morning air. The coldness of the night and the hardness of the ground had disturbed his sleep, but only for short periods and then his mind had been riddled with guilt. The man he'd seen riding off was too far away to identify, but Ben had an uneasy feeling that he might be connected with the Brogan family. Ben had shot Ike Brogan after he'd goaded Ben about being faster than him on the draw. There'd been plenty of witnesses that Ben had acted in self-defence, but Ben had taken the marshal's advice and left town. That had been just over a year ago and Ben had just drifted further and further south until he'd settled down in his job on the Hankin Ranch.

Ben had often wondered how things

might have been for him if he'd been brought up in a normal family instead of being cared for by the girls at Sandy's Saloon in Delmont Falls. He'd been abandoned by one of the saloon girls who had then killed herself. Sandy who ran the small group of girls had done most of the caring and he'd come to look on her as his ma. She'd protected him from the law after he'd shot and killed a man when he was just a boy. Ben had been nineteen years old when Sandy died and left him a small sum of money. Two days after her funeral he'd caught a train to Jolin County to start a life without painful reminders of his beloved Sandy. He'd settled in pretty well and life was good. He'd done a bit of travelling and worked for a number of ranchers for almost four years, but always ended back in Jolin County. Then he got involved with the Dooley brothers and he started drinking. That's when he started using his fists and gun for no good reason most of the time, except that he'd been taught to get in first and ask questions later. He'd had a series of barmen and lawmen as uncles, mostly friends of the girls, always giving him advice about how to look after himself when trouble came his way. Ben Oakes had no reason to fear most men, but sometimes wished he'd grown up like other boys who'd gone fishing with their pa and played with their brothers and young buddies. Sandy had once told him that Lady Luck would follow him wherever he went and when he'd settled in at the Hankin Ranch he'd thought she was right, but now luck appeared to have deserted him.

He had no particular plan except to ride into Claymore, get himself some grub, a wash and a change of clothes. He'd made a promise to Madeline that he would find Todd's killer, but now he was thinking that he had no chance of fulfilling it. He'd come across a lone rider just before he'd bedded down last night and he'd told Ben that Claymore Ridge was a good two days' ride away and the trail was rough and not an area to get lost in. The man had given him some bread when he'd asked him if he had any grub to sell and he'd refused to take any payment for it. He'd seemed uncomfortable and Ben wondered if it was because he was still showing the signs of the beating the cowhands had given before he'd been handed over to the marshal.

★ ★ ★

It was late afternoon and the burning heat had slackened off a little when Ben was preparing to make another stop. He had been in deep thought as he'd kept the horse moving at a steady trot and he was startled by the sound of a man's voice as he passed some rocks at the side of the trail.

'Howdy, mister,' the man called out, in a slow friendly drawl.

Ben pulled on the reins and returned the greeting and then spotted another man grooming a horse. The caller was at least sixty years of age. His face was red, blotchy and wrinkly. He had a roguish look, but seemed friendly enough as he invited Ben to join them for a brew of coffee. Ben was to learn that 'them' was Eli Bracken and his son who went by the name of Denzil and bore no resemblance to his pa. Denzil had a threatening look on his face and Ben figured it had seen more than its fair share of brawling. Ben noticed the bluish scar across the bridge of Denzil's nose and wondered how many times it had been broken. Someone or something must have chewed off the piece that was missing from one of his ears.

'Much obliged,' said Ben, as he accepted the invitation before he dismounted and tied the reins to the tree alongside the other two horses, one of which was unsaddled. Ben admired the palomino that Denzil had been grooming and then settled near the small fire.

'That's a fine-looking horse,' said Ben, who had never seen a palomino before, or at least not one as distinctive as this one.

'It's Denzil's pride and joy. He won it in a card game from a fancy Dan from back East. He plans to use it for breeding,' Eli explained.

Ben accepted the mug of coffee and settled himself down some distance away from the fire.

'If you're not in a hurry you are welcome to share our food when my other son, Erin, returns. We spotted a chuck-wagon on the way in and Erin's gone to buy some grub off the driver. He should've been back by now so he won't be too long. Mind you he's a bit of a dreamer and lazy with it.'

Ben had introduced himself as Sam Devine, which was his real name and safer than using Ben Oakes, the name of a wanted man.

'So, Sam, where are you heading if it ain't being too nosy?'

'I plan to leave the trail to Claymore soon and then head west to Michlow,' Ben lied, just in case anyone trailing him ran into Eli and his boys, and then added 'I hear there's lots of work there even though it's a small town; but I prefer that to somewhere like Claymore.'

'I know what you mean, but Claymore has more than its share of pretty women,' said Eli, smiling and showing a full set of fine white teeth. Maybe it was the redness of his face that made them look so. There was a moment of silence before Eli spoke again, 'What I wouldn't like to do to one of those saloon girls in Claymore if I was six months younger.'

Ben smiled, Denzil scowled and Eli chortled and then began coughing, causing his face to appear as red as a ripe tomato. When he had finally recovered he turned to Denzil.

'You'd better take my horse and go and look for your brother and tell him to get back here with the food pronto. My belly is beginning to make the sort of noise it does when it wants filling up with grub.'

'He'll be back soon, Pa,' said Denzil.

'Then you won't have to ride very far, will you, lazy-bones!'

Eli shook his head and Denzil got up and trudged his way towards Eli's sorrel that was standing next to the palomino.

Eli watched his son ride off and then said, 'That boy's never happy unless he's pampering that horse or he's fighting. Have you ever seen such a big ape of a man?'

Ben didn't reply, but the answer would have been no, although he remembered a barman at Sandy's who use to be a bare-knuckle fighter who would have been a good match for Denzil.

Ben was happy to listen to Eli's chin-wagging about his life as a travelling salesman. The conversation was non-stop and mostly one way, but it helped take Ben's mind off his troubles. Eli eventually paused for a moment and then looked serious for the first time.

'I'm getting a bit worried about my

boys taking this long,' Eli said as he poked the fire with a long branch and then turned to Ben. 'I'd like to borrow that big horse of yours, if I can climb aboard it, and go and find them. I'd saddle the palomino, but I would never hear the end of it from Denzil. He treats that horse as though it's something special, but I suppose it is to him. I wish he'd show as much interest in women as he does in that animal. I've told him that a horse isn't any use to a man on a cold night.'

Ben didn't reply immediately, thinking that if Eli and his sons didn't come back then he might be left with a stolen horse if the story about the card game was all lies. Then he reminded himself that his own horse was stolen.

Eli poked the fire again, threw the smouldering branch away and then said. 'If we don't come back I think you'll get a bargain because your horse doesn't look anything special, apart from its size. No offence, mister, but it looks a bit long in the tooth, just like me, I suppose.'

Ben had finished his deliberating and replied, 'You're welcome to borrow it, but I'll need to get moving when you get back. I'd be obliged if you would sell me some of your food before I hit the trail again.'

'There'll be enough for us all, so you can buy what you want. I'll give them another few minutes,' said Eli, but he was soon struggling to his feet and heading towards where the horses were hitched to a juniper tree. He patted the palomino and turned to Ben and said, 'What do you think the palomino is worth? I bet you've got a good eye for a horse.'

'I wouldn't like to guess what a horse like that would fetch, but I've never seen a finer-looking one.'

'Right, let me go and round up my two dozy sons,' said Eli, and mounted Ben's horse at the third attempt. 'Be back in no time, feller, so keep the coffee brewing.'

Ben watched Eli ride off and then he lay back against the small rock. The heat of the fire had him feeling drowsy and he was soon asleep.

Ben woke with a start, wondering where he was. He rubbed his eyes and the fog cleared from his brain. The fire was out and there was no sign of Eli or his sons, so Ben walked the short distance to the trail to look for them. He had a clear view but there was no sign of any riders and he decided that something had gone wrong and he should consider going looking for Eli and his boys.

The light had faded a little when Ben started saddling up the palomino, intending to head off in the direction that he watched Eli and Denzil take. If he couldn't find them soon then he would continue on his way to Claymore.

The palomino neighed as soon as he placed a foot in the stirrup and Ben wondered if it might be what some folks called a one-man horse and sensed that he wasn't Denzil. Maybe Denzil's pampering had made it that way, but he'd got the impression that Denzil had only owned it for a very short time.

'Easy,' Ben whispered, and then swung his leg over to mount the horse. He had barely rested into the saddle when the horse shook its head and neighed some more, indicating its objection. The animal seemed to be in some sort of discomfort, or maybe it was just distressed.

The horse had moved just a few feet when Ben realized why it had objected to him on its back. The animal was lame.

'Damn, damn,' Ben cursed, as he realized that he was the victim of a confidence trick carried out by a son of a bitch who called himself Eli. Denzil, or whatever his name was, might be his son, but Ben had serious doubts about there being a chuck-wagon and another son.

Ben sat down on a nearby rock and pondered what to do with the animal, but quickly decided there was no way it could be helped except to end its life with a bullet. He drew his pistol, held it against its head and pulled the trigger. The magnificent animal fell to the ground with a thud. Ben checked that it was dead, and then inspected the contents of the saddle-bags that lay close to it and discovered that they contained some smelly clothes and an even smellier piece of cheese which he intended to eat later. The no-goods who stole his horse would be in for a disappointment when they searched through its saddle-bags because the money that Madeline had given him was stuffed inside the shirt he was wearing. Ben picked up the blanket that was near the fire intending to use it later to keep out the cold night air and then drank the cold dregs from the coffee pot. He took a final look at the dead horse and then headed in the direction of Claymore Ridge with only a small piece of mouldy cheese and a few mouthfuls of water in the canteen that Eli had left behind. He hoped whatever dangers lay ahead he wouldn't be wishing he had the Winchester rifle which had been in the scabbard on the horse that Eli had taken. He intended to walk until dark, but hoped that Eli and Denzil might come looking for him.

7

Ben figured that he'd walked close to ten miles during his first day on foot before tiredness had forced him to bed down in an enclosure surrounded by small rocks. He hadn't seen a living soul, except for the odd buzzard. He had only eaten a few berries, some bread and the tiny portion of foul-smelling cheese since his meagre meal in his jail cell. Unless someone came by with some food he would have to kill something and be prepared to eat it raw because he had no means of lighting a fire.

Before Ben drifted off to sleep he remembered thinking that some of the areas he'd passed through looked familiar, even though it was mostly rocks and sand. He feared he would be dead long before he reached the water he badly needed. Probably his best hope of survival was if he met a fellow traveller, or Eli and son. He'd wondered how they'd come about the palomino and whether they'd used a similar trick before. If Ben could be granted two wishes then the first would have been to find water and food. The second would be to meet up with Eli and his son one day when he had the strength to settle a score with them for leaving him to die. His final thought before he fell asleep was that he should have tried to rip some flesh from the palomino before he'd left it for the buzzards.

* * *

Ben had managed some sleep in the soft sand despite the coldness of the night and at first light he decided to start walking, hoping to cover some distance before the sun burned into his clothes and skin. His mouth was already dry and tasted foul. He cleared his throat and tried to spit into the sand, hoping to clear the legacy of yesterday's cheese, but his mouth was too dry. He had a griping pain in his stomach and, when he touched his forehead, it felt as though it was on fire.

Come midday when the sun was high in the sky he started to stagger as he approached the small group of boulders, hoping that one of them was tall enough for him to shelter from the sun. His feet were aching, but the griping pain in his stomach had gone and he was certain that his temperature was normal for anyone in these conditions and not the start of some fever or other illness. He placed the blanket on the ground behind the rock that provided some shelter and settled down to rest. Sleep didn't come easy despite his tiredness. He'd removed his boots and could feel the throbbing pain from his blisters. He was having doubts about whether he'd made a mistake by not heading back towards Tremaine Creek. At least he would have stood more chance of finding water, but he would have risked running into whoever might come after him. Unless his luck changed he knew he was going to die alone and be forever branded a murderer.

★ ★ ★

He didn't know how long he'd slept, but the sun was low in the sky now. The blisters had stopped throbbing, but his legs felt itchy. He rolled up his pants and scratched and scratched before he inspected his legs and discovered that they were covered in tiny bites. Some of the culprits were still inside his pants. He'd never seen insects this big before and figured they were some kind of ant. They were red in colour, or were they smeared with his blood! He jumped up and tried to brush them from his legs, then he felt the itchiness on his upper body and was soon stripped naked, desperate to brush his tiny attackers away.

'Jesus,' he howled, when he saw the

bite marks on most parts of his body. It seemed that only his manhood had not been a target. It took many minutes of shaking his clothes and then banging them against the rocks before he decided that the last pesky insect had been removed.

He dressed and had almost forgotten to shake out his boots, but when he did there were no insects in there, just a small lizard. He was slow in responding as it scurried away, but managed to grab it when it had perched on the small rock. The little devil didn't know it, but its species had just met a new predator. He held it firmly in one hand and secured its head in between two fingers of his other hand and twisted its neck. Ben opened his hand and inspected the dead lizard. He felt the creature's body and decided that he shouldn't encounter anything too hard for his teeth to handle, but it was too big to stuff into his mouth whole and he had nothing to cut it up with.

'Here goes,' he said and steeled himself before he bit off the lizard's head and began chewing it furiously while his eyes were closed tightly. He swallowed the result of his first chewing and he quickly took another bite, but this time it was a struggle before he finally tore away the next mouthful. He discarded the tail, the only part that he hadn't eaten and wiped his hand across his mouth. He'd decided against licking his lips, but he did scour the nearby rocks hoping to find another one to provide him with some nourishment and any tiny amount of liquid that his body needed and craved. He was out of luck and he wondered if the little feller's companions had witnessed its unlikely end.

It was time to get moving and he lifted the blanket from the ground and shook it causing yet more ants to be scattered. Then he saw the moving carpet of his tormentors on the ground. He had been bedded down on their nest and they had clearly not liked his intrusion. He spread the blanket back on the ground near the nest and scooped the ants on to the blanket and then folded it so they were trapped inside. He placed the folded blanket on one of the rocks and then used the handle of his pistol to gently tap in the area where they were trapped. If he could eat a lizard then he was sure that that he could manage a mouthful of squashed insects. When he unfurled the blanket he discovered that a few had survived and some scurried for freedom, while others were too stunned or weak and he quashed those between his fingers. He scooped the dead ants into his hand and then licked them into his mouth. The taste was bitter and some stuck between his teeth along with the bits of sand that had been scooped up. He preferred the lizard, but before he left he ate a second helping of squashed ants.

★　★　★

The light was fading and his blistered feet had stopped him from making much progress when he saw the dead carcass ahead which two buzzards were devouring, but they scattered when he got closer. Any hope that it might provide him with some food disappeared when the foul smell hit his nostrils. He wasn't ready to eat decayed flesh of the wolf, at least not yet. He walked on for only a short while before he bedded down for the night with the consolation that the carcass of the wolf suggested that there must be water not too far away and that meant vegetation and a supply of food that would be more appealing than what he'd sampled today.

★   ★   ★

Ben shielded his eyes from the bright sun as he tried opening them. He was hungry, his mouth was parched and he felt dog tired despite his long sleep. He had no inclination to raise his stiffened body and closed his eyes again, but they were soon opened when he sensed the shadow briefly pass over.

'Damn,' he cursed, when he saw the two buzzards fly upwards and out of pistol range. Maybe if he kept perfectly still they would come back, but he figured they were too cunning to fall for that. He felt like an old man as he struggled to his feet due to the stiffness and weakness of his muscles. Maybe he should have stayed closer to the carcass he'd come across then he might have stood a chance of shooting a buzzard as it fed on the remains of the wolf. He prayed that his luck would change soon along with the terrain. At least he was able to use the blanket to act as a hood and help keep the sun off his face.

*   *   *

He'd been treading wearily along the dusty trails when he saw the rocks and hills in the distance. At least they would provide some shelter and the possibility of food and water, but it was water that he needed most. If he didn't find it by this time tomorrow then he wouldn't make it, he was sure of that.

At times he'd felt he was walking on the spot and not really progressing at all and it was mid afternoon when he reached the base of the small hills. They hadn't seemed that far away, but at one point they didn't seem to be getting any closer. He passed his tongue over his dried lips, and took a deep breath before he headed for the passage between the small hills. The shaded enclosure brought some instant relief from the hot sun, but he faltered when he heard the unmistakable sound of a horse snorting.

'In here,' he heard the croaky voice call out.

Ben drew his pistol even though the call had sounded more like an invitation than a threat. He wondered if it might be Eli up to his old tricks, but he decided it wasn't.

'Howdy. I'm coming in,' Ben called

out, and then headed towards a gap between some rocks. He saw the horse first and then the old-timer who was lying with his back to the rocks with a blanket wrapped around him.

'You won't need that gun, young feller. I ain't going to put up a fight if you want to take anything.'

Ben holstered his gun, apologized and then explained that the last person he'd met ended up stealing his horse and he wasn't in a trusting mood.

'I'm sorry to hear that, son, because anyone out here without a horse is likely to end their days in this Godforsaken place and that's a fact. If you're a stranger to these parts you might not know that we're in what's known as the Dead Bones Hills.'

Ben took a closer look at the man who was one of the oldest looking he'd ever seen. He had a bushy white beard, a skinny face and no teeth that Ben could see.

'What happened to you, mister?' Ben asked, when he saw the dried blood and deep gouges on the man's face.

'Sit yourself down and I'll tell you, but you look as though you'll want to take a drink of water from that canteen over there.' The man gestured towards a canteen near the rocks and there was another one next to him.

'Much obliged,' said Ben as he reached for the canteen, anticipating the moment when he'd lose the dryness in his mouth.

'Make sure that you sip it slowly even though you want to gulp it. Savour it as though it's the last drop of water you'll ever taste,' advised the man.

'Are you sure you can spare it?' said Ben, not expecting the man to say no, but not expecting his reply either.

'There's not much water left. I've made sure that Betty over there's had enough, but I won't need any where I'm going.'

Ben wondered what the old-timer meant by his remarks. He unscrewed the top of the canteen, but before he lifted it to his mouth he offered his hand to the man and introduced himself as Sam Devine.

The man lifted his hand from beneath the blanket and Ben winced as he shook the bloodstained hand that had two fingers missing.

'Joel Monk, pleased to meet you. And you ought to know that this is my best hand. I had argument with that son of a bitch over there.'

Ben delayed his long awaited reunion with water and looked in the direction that Joel had nodded towards and saw the handle of a knife that had been buried to the hilt in the creature's throat.

'In case you've never seen one before, it's a mountain lion,' Joel said, then added 'It jumped me as I rode by a few days ago. Plumb scared the shit out of my old horse, Betty, over there, and me, for that matter. There I was thinking of sitting in a saloon with a nice cool beer and it pounced without a sound and knocked me off Betty. I still don't know how I managed to get my knife out and kill the bugger. I bet it got the shock of his life when I stuck my knife in its gizzard and managed to twist it, but it still did me some damage. So this blood you can see isn't all mine.' Joel laughed while Ben took a gulp of water, forgetting the advice he'd been given to sip it slowly. He cherished the moment as the surprisingly cool liquid took away the burning dryness at the back of his throat. Ben sighed with a mixture of pleasure and relief.

'You were mighty lucky to escape with just damaged hands. If you've got some cloth I could try bandaging those for you.'

'I wasn't that lucky, son,' said Joel, and pulled back the blanket to reveal his blood-soaked clothing.

'Jesus,' Ben gasped, when he saw the badly mauled flesh. The bottom half of one leg wouldn't have been out of place in a butcher's shop or slaughterhouse. The other hand that had been hidden by the blanket had only just a small piece of each finger left.

Joel managed a weak smile before he spoke. 'Just as well we have hard bones, or you'd be looking at a one-legged man right now. I still used to like dancing even at my age, but those days are over for me. I've been thinking of me and old Myrtle Jacks at the barn dance in Sanluca, just last spring.'

'Is there anything I can do to ease your pain and make you more comfortable?' Ben offered again.

'It's not as bad as it looks, but if the pain bothers me then I just take a swig of my home-made whiskcy, although that's running low, just like the water. I'd appreciate it if you'd start up a fire and brew us some coffee, and there's some food in those bags over there. And I'd be much obliged if you could give me my knife back and drag that carcass away from here. It's beginning to reek and I'm thinking its smell is worse than its bite.' Joel burst into laughter at his own joke, before he began coughing. He cleared his throat with a grunt and then spat into the sand then said, 'You might want to cut us a few juicy steaks from its hind.'

Joel saw the look on Ben's face and added, 'I'm only joking, son. I tried it once some years ago and it isn't something I'd want to try again unless it stopped me from dying of starvation. If you find any other wounds on him then the creature I heard last night must have come in here and ripped away a few chunks. I only hope it wasn't a relative of that one.'

Ben gripped the handle of the knife, pulled it free and cleaned the blade before handing it to Joel. The old-timer must have been one gutsy feller to get the better of the lion which was much heavier and larger upon closer inspection. The wounds on its body were crawling with maggots, and, as Joel had surmised, chunks of flesh had been ripped from its belly.

As they sat eating the beans and dried bread that Ben had prepared, Joel told him that he'd been prospecting for silver in a disused mine just off the main trail a couple of miles from here. He'd found just one small piece that would have just about paid for a good night's drinking in a saloon and maybe a month's supply of baccy. He had been on his way back to his home in Sanluca when the lion planned to have him for its dinner.

When Ben mentioned his plans to head for Claymore Ridge the old-timer shook his head and said, 'You'd never make it on foot to Sanluca, never mind Claymore, but you might if you take my old horse.'

'You mean so I could go and get some help, perhaps bring a doctor to patch you up.'

Joel gave a weak smile, 'There's no one who can help me son, but you can save yourself. I'm not afraid of dying, because I've had me a good life and been blessed with good fortune until now. The only thing that scares the shit out of me is the thought of being plucked at by the buzzards. I've seen their leftovers a few times and it weren't a pretty sight. I once came across a family that must have strayed off the trail and got lost. They were a young couple with a pretty little blonde-haired girl of no more than seven years old. I managed to bury their remains, but I can still picture how they were even though I turned my eyes away after seeing them for a few seconds. I know it sounds silly, but if there is another place we go to after we die then I'd like to have my eyes still intact and if it don't sound too crude I'd like to have my manhood in one piece as well. There's no point in going to heaven if you haven't got the bits to enjoy it.'

Ben smiled at Joel and marvelled at how the old-timer could make jokes despite his obvious pain. If there was some way of getting Joel to where he could be helped then Ben was determined to do it. He told Joel that if he could guide him to some water then they might make it. He could strap Joel to his horse and lead it Sanluca.

'There's water less than two miles

from here, but in the opposite direction to Sanluca which is thirty or more. Sanluca is this side of Claymore where you're heading, but I wouldn't make it there and I'd slow you down. I tell you what; let's talk about it some more in the morning. Perhaps I might be feeling stronger after that meal. Just get me an extra blanket from over there and take one for yourself.'

Ben handed Joel the blanket and asked, 'Do you think there might be more critters about?' Ben was wondering if he would be best staying awake if he didn't want to end up like Joel.

'There might be,' replied Joel. 'I brought some city folks up to these parts a couple of years ago. One of them was real educated and had studied the mountain lion. He told me that it can be found in just about any terrain and not just in the mountains like most folks think. But he reckoned that the creature is a loner and stays within its own territory. I'm not sure what happens during the mating season though. In case you hadn't noticed, my attacker was a female and there could be some young ones about. Maybe I was going to be a family meal. Best build the fire up before you bed down and keep your pistol handy. Goodnight, young feller. Oh, I nearly forgot to tell you how to get to the water which is close to where I did my bit of prospecting. As I already mentioned it's in the opposite direction to Claymore Ridge, but that's where you'll have to head if you want to stay alive. You don't really have a choice.'

Ben listened carefully as Joel explained the directions to the river, but Joel started repeating himself and then there were pauses until he began snoring loudly. He was still snoring long after Ben had bedded down. It had been a stroke of luck stumbling upon old Joel. Now his belly wasn't screaming for food and the dryness had left his mouth. He was determined that what-ever happened tomorrow, he wasn't going to leave the old-timer to die on his own. He just hoped that should any lion cubs come calling during the night looking for their ma they would be small ones. He took Joel's advice and made sure that his pistol was close at hand. Before he went to sleep he made a mental note to ask Joel if he might know Eli and his son Denzil. They may have used false names, but they made an odd-looking pair and might be known in these parts.

★   ★   ★

Come morning it took Ben a while to get his bearings and then remember where he was. He turned towards Joel's horse and saw that it was pawing at the ground making a steady noise. Perhaps that was what had woken him up, but it hadn't disturbed old Joel. Ben gathered the wood together and soon had the fire going. He waited for the coffee to be brewed before he ventured over to where Joel was and then realized that the nice old-timer had drunk his last cup of coffee. Joel was dead, his opened eyes staring towards the sky. His knife lay beside him, having fallen from his grasp. Ben grimaced when he saw the gaping wound. Joel had slit his own throat. Ben leaned on one knee and closed Joel's eyes. His skin was cold and Ben wondered if he had faked his snoring and then killed himself as soon as Ben had drifted off to sleep. He had no doubt that Joel's decision to end his life had been for his benefit. He'd wanted to try and help the old-timer and now the only way he could do that was to give him a decent burial. Ben had seen a shovel and a pickaxe, obviously used by Joel during his prospecting, so he would have no trouble burying Joel deep so that his body was safe from any scavengers that might pass this way. He had no idea what sort of life Joel had led, but he would have bet his last dollar that it would have been a good and honest one.

* ★ ★

It was mid morning by the time Ben had buried Joel, and gathered some of the old-timer's belongings together. He felt sad as he left the enclosure on Joel's horse and wondered how far old Betty would take him, but it seemed a sturdy enough animal and at least there wouldn't be the weight of the pickaxe, shovel and other bits that he must have carried. Ben was soon encouraged by the strength of the horse and he was able to make good progress in the direction of where he hoped he would find the river.

Joel had mentioned there being some caves on the right of the trail and Ben was beginning to think he'd not followed the directions until he saw them in the distance. He urged the horse on and it immediately swerved off the trail as though objecting to his demand for extra speed. 'Easy,' said Ben, as he pulled on the reins to slow it down and at the same time steer it back onto the narrow trail. Then he saw the reason for the horse's diversion. It was a large headed snake which was now just six feet in front of him. Ben elected to draw his pistol rather than take avoiding action and fired into the head of the hissing reptile. Ben was almost unsaddled as the blast of the gun close to its ear spooked Betty who surged forward into a wild gallop.

He let the horse slow down in its own time and then gradually urged it on. When they were moving at a steady pace he leaned forward and said, 'I promise I won't do that again.'

★   ★   ★

Ben had been musing about what sort of life Joel might have led and it seemed no time at all when he heard the sound of the flowing river before he saw it. It was just about the most welcoming sound he had ever heard. He directed Betty through a small gap in the trees and opted to lead the horse down the gentle slope towards the fast flowing river below. He guessed he couldn't be too far from the disused mine where Joel had found his small piece of silver. Ben had heard many tales of men getting rich overnight by striking it lucky and of others whose luck had been short lived when they had been killed by those who wanted to steal their stake.

Ben doubted if he would ever forget the pleasure he felt as he stripped off and bathed in the fresh water and scooped up handfuls of it to drink. Betty slurped the welcome liquid with equal relish. Ben had never fished before, but was wishing he had because he'd seen a couple of large fish leap out of the water and then disappear. He filled up the three canteens that he'd brought and picked some fruit from the trees. The first sample he tried of the small green fruit tasted bitter, but most of those that followed were sweet enough to enjoy. He had no idea what the fruit was called, but just hoped that it wasn't poisonous.

It would be some hours before it was dark, but Ben decided to camp by the water. Joel's horse had done well today and had eaten some short grass, and Ben was confident that they would be able to reach Sanluca by early afternoon tomorrow. Joel hadn't mentioned that he had kin in the town, but Ben was sure that Myrtle would know if he had any.

Ben was in no particular hurry to reach Claymore Ridge and it would ease his conscience if he could tell someone about Joel's demise and hand over some of his belongings, including a small amount of money. He also wanted to buy the horse or hand it over and purchase another one.

★ ★ ★

Come early morning Ben was regretting his decision to bed down near the trees because an assortment of bird sounds had him waking up earlier than he intended.

Betty seemed even stronger after the night's rest and it didn't seem long before they passed the spot where Joel was laid to rest. Ben was saddened, but he didn't linger and heeled Betty in the direction of Sanluca. He was soon realizing the wisdom of Joel's advice to back-track for water when the terrain became almost desert-like again.

By early afternoon the scenery changed dramatically. He was thinking that if he had reached this far on foot he could have survived. The luscious-ness of the grass reminded him of the Hankin range and he wondered if Madeline had done like he'd suggested and not got into trouble over his escape. Milton Hankin would be offering a reward for his capture and the man who'd planned to burn down his cell would be disappointed that Ben had escaped and would probably be leading the lynch mob, determined to hunt him down. Ben had spent some time wondering about the bastard, but he had no idea who he might be.

8

Ben had been to a few of what folks described as a one-horse town, but his first impression of Sanluca was that they didn't come any smaller than this. On his ride down Main Street he counted just half-a-dozen buildings, with three on either side. Ben directed the horse towards Ma Kent's Saloon which had the undertakers on one side and Jethro's Store on the other. He guided his horse to the hitch rail outside the saloon and eased himself out of the saddle, still suffering from the stiffness from his long walks. This side of the street was in the shade so the animal would be all right while he quenched his thirst on a beer and maybe filled his belly with some real food.

'Where did you get that horse, mister?' called out the man whom Ben had just spotted sitting on a bench on the side-walk. Ben was about to tell him to mind his own goddamn business when Ben saw that he was wearing a deputy marshal's badge. Ben leapt onto the sidewalk, while drawing his pistol. The man looked puzzled and had started to rise from the bench as Ben pistol whipped him either side of his face. The man was dazed, and struggling to get up from the bench when Ben heaved him up by his hair and delivered a vicious blow to the man's belly and then hurled into the dusty street. He was about to rush down the steps and inflict more pain on the shocked and winded man, but Ben's intention to beat him into unconsciousness was halted when a voice roared out from across the street, 'Stay where you are, mister.'

Ben looked in the direction of the caller who was standing outside the marshal's office and was pointing a rifle at him.

'Put your hands above your head and step down into the street,' the marshal ordered as he walked towards Ben. The marshal's face wore a grim expression and Ben had already decided that this lawman wouldn't hesitate to pull the trigger of his rifle if Ben tried anything, so he followed the marshal's order to drop his pistol and raise his hands above his head.

'I watched you ride in, mister, and attack him for no reason that I could see. Well, I don't tolerate brawling in my town. So you'll be getting a spell across the street in one of my cells unless he stole your wife or your old grandma's purse. I can tell you that the cells weren't designed for comfort. If the rats don't bite you while you sleep then the bugs certainly will.'

'That deputy is a no-good horse thief,' replied Ben, nodding in the direction of the man who was now kneeling in the dusty street and looked to be in some pain.

'What deputy?' asked the marshal, while eying Ben as though he was some sort of idiot.

'That one,' replied Ben, nodding his head once again towards the man who was now rubbing his shoulder. 'Him and his pa, Eli, stole my horse and left me with a lame animal to die in the desert.'

'Why are you calling him a deputy?' asked the marshal, his face still showing a look of bewilderment.

'Because, the sly no-good was wearing a badge and must have taken it off.'

Ben was relieved when the marshal addressed the man as Denzil and ordered him to empty his pockets.

Denzil looked sheepish when he took the badge from his shirt pocket and said, 'It was just a bit of fun, Marshal. I've always wanted to be a deputy.'

'Impersonating an officer of the law isn't fun. Now you get your dumb ass across the street. You'll be joining your brain-sizzled pa in the cells until I decide what to do with you both.'

The marshal turned to Ben. 'You can lower your hands, mister, but Denzil and his pa may not be the only horse-thieves because, if I'm not mistaken, that horse you rode in on doesn't belong to you. You'd better come across the street and tell me how you come to be riding Joel Monk's horse and if you tell me you found it running loose, then I'll lock you up.'

Marshal Henry Aber was fifty-two years old. His bushy moustache was snow white and his pale-blue eyes didn't blink too often. The marshal wasn't as heavily built as Denzil, but he still outweighed Ben and most men. Once he'd locked Denzil in a cell next to his pa he asked Ben to explain how he came to be in possession of Joel Monk's horse and listened intently to Ben's reply.

'Well that's a real damn shame, mister. By the way, what name do you go by? I don't suppose you're about to tell me your real name, or one that's on that pile of Wanted posters over there.'

'They call me Sam Devine. That's my real name and to save you asking, Marshal, I'm heading out of here as soon as I've got some things together, had me a meal and handed over Joel's belongings.'

The marshal sighed and shook his head. 'A lot of people will be sad to hear about Joel. He was one hell of a character and will be missed around here. Life can be cruel at times, but varmints like Eli Bracken and his son seem to escape tragedy. The longer I'm in this job the more I realize that there's no justice in this damned world of ours. All that stuff that we hear every Sunday from the preacher about following the ways of God is a load of bullshit.'

Marshal Aber said that Joel had no kinfolk. His wife Alice had died ten years or more ago and they never had any children.

'What's going to happen to his belongings, Marshal? I brought a few bits and pieces and the few dollars he had with him. They're in his saddle-bag. I need to know who to hand them over to along with his horse.'

Marshal Aber scratched his head and

looked thoughtful for a moment before he replied, 'The way I see it, mister, is that old Joel wanted you to have his horse and probably anything else. You gave him a decent burial and you came here looking for any kinfolk and that makes you an honest sort of feller in my book. You keep Joel's horse. It's the simplest solution.'

Ben explained how Eli and Denzil had tricked him and stole his horse leaving him with the lame palomino which he had to put out of its misery.

The marshal sighed and said 'Those two might not have been blessed with much in the way of brains, but they are a cunning pair of bastards, or at least Eli is and Denzil is his stooge. I'm afraid Eli sold your horse if it's the one he brought into town the other day and he's probably spent most of the money on drink. That's why he's locked up because he made such a nuisance of himself.'

Ben asked what would happen to the horse-thieves and the marshal smiled.

'I've got a plan for them which will mean that they won't be causing any problems around here in the future.'

'Will they be going to prison?' Ben asked. He was eager to know what sort of suffering they would face, hoping it would be long and painful.

'No, that would involve me in paperwork and maybe a lot of expense for the town. So, I'm going to let them stew in the cells for a few days and then let them go.'

Ben was thinking that it didn't seem much of a punishment and then the marshal explained that Eli and Denzil had stolen the palomino from someone named Titus Lennox. It was part of Lennox's prize breeding stock and he'd offered a reward for anyone who turned the thieves in. The marshal intended telling Eli that if he and Denzil ever stepped out of line he would tell Lennox what they'd done. They would know that as sure as night follows day, Titus Lennox would have them hunted down and they would

113

end up hanging from a tree.

Ben told the marshal he planned to buy some new clothes, food supplies and have one king-sized meal at the diner next door to the marshal's office before he went looking for Myrtle Jacks to tell her about Joel. The marshal told him that he'd find her across the street helping out at the general store. They both agreed that it was best to tell Myrtle that Joel had just passed away peacefully and spare her the gory details. Ben declined the marshal's offer to be there when he told Myrtle.

Ben had his meal, visited the barber's shop and then headed for the general store. He bought his supplies and clothes before he passed on the news to the homely-looking Myrtle. There were tears in her eyes when he recounted Joel telling him about their dancing and more tears when he gave her the small piece of silver that Joel had found during his final day of prospecting. She told Ben that she would treasure it until her dying day because Joel had intended to marry her on his return from his last trip away. He'd planned to settle down at the ripe old age of seventy-two years of age.

* * *

Ben rode out of Sanluca, leaving behind a lovely but sad lady and two varmints who had left him to die. Ben was thinking that if he passed a sign to the Titus Lennox ranch he might just be tempted to tell him the whereabouts of the horse-thieves he was looking for.

9

It was close to sun-up by the time Ben started the slow ride down Claymore's Main Street after a long, but uneventful ride from Sanluca.

Ben had heard people talk about Claymore Ridge and how it had changed, but it didn't look anything special to him apart from its size. He was hoping that once he was here it might jog his memory, but so far it hadn't. It had at least one of about every shop and establishment, including John Moorcroft's barber's shop which had a closed sign outside and a notice that explained that he'd *Gone Painting*. Ben had heard of folks going fishing, but not painting. The Merton Hotel looked a bit grand for his liking, but he intended booking in there later.

The town was teaming with people and an assortment of carriages being driven along the street. Most of the buildings were solidly built, including the white wooden chapel that stood next to the courthouse. The Claymore Central Bank was impressive with its twin pillars and there were two black-suited guards outside the entrance, both carrying rifles, their long coats pushed to one side to reveal their Colt pistols. The men had identical black moustaches that curled up at the ends. Ben was thinking they must be brothers, perhaps even twins.

By the time he reached the livery at the other end of the town he'd received a mixture of glances from folk passing by. They ranged from friendly to hostile, with the odd curious glance and a smile from a young woman who was leaving the hotel.

The man who ran the livery wasn't exactly talkative as Ben arranged and paid for Betty to be fed and stabled for the night. He gave Ben a surprised look when he asked if he could use the water trough in the corral at the back to clean himself up, but he grudgingly agreed. As Ben was leaving, the livery man told him that the town had three hotels and two barber shops, one of which had bathing facilities.

Ben made his way down Main Street in the direction of the Derby Saloon which had looked like one of the newer buildings in town. He remembered someone saying that the town's saloons had only opened this past year because previously the town council had been against the idea, fearing it would attract undesirables to the town. Ben guessed that once the railroad had arrived they didn't have much option. As Ben mounted the sidewalk outside the saloon, the man sitting on the bench near the door looked him up and down as though checking him over. Maybe he was some kind of doorman? That thought was quickly dismissed when he stood up and Ben realized that he was the marshal.

'This is a peaceful town, mister, and we aim to keep it that way. Bear that in mind if you intend filling yourself full of liquor. My name is Slaney and I hope we don't meet up again.'

Ben was bemused by the remarks and was tempted to make some comment, but kept himself in check. The marshal was about forty years old, had a droopy black moustache and his dark eyes were cold. He was on the tall side and, as he walked away, Ben noticed that he had a severe limp, maybe the result of an old bullet wound.

Ben pushed open the swing doors of the saloon and made his way inside. The air was partly clouded by tobacco smoke, but it didn't stop him getting a whiff of some strong scent. It was coming from the girl who'd smiled at him earlier near the hotel and she did so again.

'You look like you need some company, stranger,' she said. Ben's eyes drifted to her low-cut, tight-fitting dress. She leaned forward, making sure that he got a good look at her exposed flesh. But Ben had other things on his mind and in any case he had no intention of sleeping with her. The girl was certainly attractive and might have looked like Madeline before the face had become hardened by her work.

'So you've come back for more, handsome,' said the dark-haired woman, who had just come down the stairs, and then warned, 'Hands off, Louise! He's mine.'

Louise looked disappointed and she said, 'Sorry, Suzanne,' then walked away.

'You haven't forgotten me already? That's not very flattering for a girl even though it was more than a few months ago. You must remember!'

Ben studied Suzanne as she took a long drag on her cigarette. She must have been in her late thirties and he guessed that she was in charge of the girls, or even the owner of the saloon. He'd seen lots of women like her, but he told her that she must have mistaken him for someone else because it was his first time in Claymore Ridge. He didn't know why he'd denied being here before because, according to Todd, he had. It had just seemed the natural thing to say.

'Don't be shy, honey. I remember you and you've got nothing to be ashamed of. I might not recall any of the names, but I never forget a face. As I've already said it's not very flattering if you really have forgotten me after such a short time.'

Ben smiled and suggested, 'Maybe it was in another town.'

Suzanne smiled at him and said, 'If you say so, honey. By the way, what do they call you?'

'Ben, Ben Oakes,' he replied, deliberately using the name.

'Ben Oakes! Now that name sure rings a bell, but I don't know why,' said Suzanne, pursing her lips as though concentrating hard to remember where she'd heard the name before.

The barman had been listening to their conversation, but with no particular interest because he'd gotten used to the girls trying every angle to entice their customers upstairs and part with their money. Now he studied the young stranger talking to Suzanne because the name sure meant something to him.

Ben offered to buy Suzanne a drink, having decided that perhaps she might help fill in a few gaps and tell him about the man she'd mistaken him for.

The barman wasn't the only man who had been interested to hear the name Ben Oakes and when Ben and Suzanne made their way to one of the tables he hurried out of the saloon.

Suzanne seemed happy with her drink and was confident that Ben would be spending more of his money on her later. At least she hoped so because things had been pretty quiet around the town since the last cattle drive had passed through.

Ben said that one of his buddies was supposed to meet up with him in Claymore and he asked if anyone had been enquiring about him.

'I told you, honey, I'm not much

good with names, but there's definitely something about yours. It'll come to me, but I can't put my finger on it right now.'

Ben had his back to the door and it was Suzanne looking over his shoulder that had him easing his hand towards his pistol, just as he heard the gun behind him being cocked.

'Put your hands on the table, mister.'

'He's doing no harm, Marshal. We're just having a quiet drink,' pleaded Suzanne, eager to keep her only hope of some business until the bar filled up later.

'You've been having a quiet drink with the man who raped Josie Webster.'

Marshal Claude Slaney reached down, pulled Ben's pistol from its holster and then prodded him in the back while ordering him to stand up. Ben pleaded his innocence and told the marshal he had never met anyone who went by the name of Josie and repeated his claim that he'd never been to Claymore before today. The marshal said that he'd had a hunch about Ben being trouble when he'd spoken to him earlier.

'Have you seen this lowlife in town before?' the marshal asked Suzanne.

'Hmm,' Suzanne sighed. 'I have, but this guy's no rapist. I just know he isn't. You get to have an instinct about these things in my line of work. Now I could tell you about some of the so called pillars of the community who go to church every Sunday and whose wives don't suspect a thing. One or two of those model citizens are more likely to rape anything in a dress than this sweet young feller.'

The marshal frowned. 'I'm not asking you for a character reference, Suzanne, and I don't see why you're trying to defend him when he's lying about never being in town before. You might want to ask yourself why he did that because I'm sure the jury will be asking themselves that question.'

Suzanne just shrugged her shoulders and then lit another cigarette. She wished the marshal would relax once in a while. He was a good-looking man, but as far as she knew he didn't pay women much attention which she found strange. Maybe one day she would entice him upstairs. She'd even be prepared to offer him a special rate on account of him helping to keep the peace and sorting out problems in the saloon.

The marshal was feeling uncomfortable at the way Suzanne seemed to be studying him and he turned away and addressed Ben. 'Start heading for the door, mister, and then across the street to my office because I'm locking you up and sending for Josie Webster to come and identify you.'

When Ben reached the marshal's office he was thinking that someone had cast a evil spell on him or he was in the middle of a nightmare. He'd come to find Todd's killer and now he was in fresh trouble. The marshal seemed a reasonable enough man, unlike Lenny Tuke, his deputy, who pushed Ben towards the cells. Ben couldn't decide on Tuke's age, but figured he was around thirty. One side of his face was badly scarred with burn marks and the eye on that side was almost closed. It looked as though he'd tried to grow a beard, but it was just patchy stubble. His black hair was greasy and, judging by his body odour, he didn't spend too much time washing, or he must sleep near his horse. Ben wondered if Tuke was sweet on the girl, Josie, or maybe a relative because he made his feelings towards Ben clear when he delivered a vicious blow to the small of Ben's back and then pushed him to the floor of the cell. Ben found it small consolation when he discovered that his cell was bigger and more comfortable than the one in Tremaine Creek.

Tuke had slammed the cell door shut and headed back to the office area, but he was back in no time at all and scowled at Ben when he said, 'The marshal said that it's too late to get Josie now, so you'll be our guest at least until tomorrow. I wouldn't worry about

126

standing trial because if she identifies you there are plenty of folks in this town who'll make sure that your lusting days are over. They'll take a knife to your balls before they string you up.'

Ben smiled at Tuke while looking him in the eye and then asked, 'I don't suppose there's much chance of me getting a nice juicy steak and couple of cold beers sent in.' Ben continued smiling, hoping he might annoy the deputy. He wasn't going to get any favours off this ugly bully who looked as though it would take something special to make him smile, except maybe someone else's pain.

'So you're a smart arse as well as a rapist. Well, we'll see how long you can keep up your wisecracks, mister, but I'll wager it won't be for long. Prime steaks are off today's menu, but I will be bringing you a little treat in the morning. Sweet dreams, cowboy.'

10

Sleep hadn't come easily to Ben, more because of his troubled mind than the coughing and puking from one of the drunks in the next cell, but he was on the point of drifting off when Tuke rattled the bars of his cell.

'Scum like you don't deserve to be fed, but the marshal ordered me, so here it is.'

Tuke pushed the small plate of beans and dry bread under the bottom of the cell bars and said that he'd bring him some coffee later. He walked away from the cell, but turned back and said, 'I might have accidentally spit on those beans. Well, accidentally on purpose, if you know what I mean, and I might just piss in your coffee before I bring it.' Tuke was in danger of having a convulsion as he laughed on his way back to the main office area.

Ben was too hungry to worry about what Tuke might have done to his meagre food ration and he was soon mopping up the remains of the beans with the bread. He was licking his lips so as not to waste a morsel when the marshal arrived with his coffee, looking a mite upset. In fact he looked even more hostile than Tuke had done.

'You have a visitor, Oakes, but it isn't a social call.'

Ben took a gulp from the tin mug and stood, wondering who the visitor might be. He doubted if it was the girl Josie because the marshal would have said so. The marshal had given a final look of disgust before he returned to the office, but Ben's visitor who had been beckoned in by the marshal displayed no real emotion, until he gave a smile of satisfaction. Ben glanced down at the empty holster. He figured the marshal must have made him leave his pistol in the office, so at least Dexter Hankin couldn't shoot him.

Dexter Hankin hadn't wanted to

come to Claymore Ridge. He had cursed his sister when she'd confessed to helping Ben escape and for telling their pa that Oakes was heading for Claymore. But now he was here and he didn't have to confront Oakes, things might work out just fine for him. He would take Oakes back to Tremaine Creek and redeem himself with his pa. Milton Hankin was a man who believed in family honour and an eye for eye. Dexter might be more of a hero if he took home a dead Ben Oakes and claimed that he'd tried to escape during the journey back to Tremaine Creek.

'Dexter, I didn't kill your brother. Madeline knows that and I'm hoping you feel the same,' said Ben. He'd never realized that the fun-loving Dexter had a serious side to him and the earlier smile had been replaced with a stern expression.

'My sister's a silly girl. Pa believes that you killed him and so do I. The marshal's back there now deliberating whether to turn you over to me so I can take you back to face trial in Tremaine Creek. He said that you were facing a serious charge here, but I guess it's not as serious as cold-blooded murder.'

'How did you know I was here? If Madeline told you, then you'll know that I came here after Todd's killer. I don't know what you've heard, Dexter, but I'm telling you again that I didn't shoot Todd.'

'You were practically caught red-handed and no one else saw this mysterious rider that you claim to have seen. Then you get my sister involved by sweet talking her. I had to check this place out and when I mentioned your name over at the saloon the barman told me that you were in the cells. So what is this serious charge you're in here for?'

Ben was on the point of explaining when the marshal appeared and a young woman was with him. She was pretty, and although barely a woman, was showing the early signs that she was with child. She looked nervous and didn't appear to hear the calming words of the marshal as she pointed her finger and screamed, 'It was him. That's Ben Oakes and it was him.' She tried to rush forward, but the marshal restrained her.

'Take it easy honey. Now this is important. Are you absolutely certain he's the man who violated you?'

'It's him,' she screeched, and then tears flooded down her face.

'What's all this about and what's this crazy girl accusing me of?' asked a shocked Dexter Hankin.

Marshal Slaney shook his head and surveyed Hankin and Oakes. Both men were about the same height and their hair colouring was the same from what he could see under Hankin's hat. The marshal asked his deputy to take Josie over to the diner, calm her down and then take her home.

Marshal Slaney scratched his head and said, 'I don't know what the hell's going on here, Hankin, but I'm arresting you for the rape of Josie Webster, now get into that cell.' The marshal nodded in the direction of the open cell next to Ben's and then added, 'I'd better keep you two apart, I suppose.'

Dexter was protesting when the marshal pulled out his pistol and said, 'Now shut your damn mouth and move. You may not have the right name, but that girl claims you raped her. That means you're going to stand trial and in case you don't know, in this town that means you'll face a hanging if the jury believes Josie Webster. Some folks say that she's got the face of an angel, so I don't think much of your chances.'

The marshal secured Dexter in the cell and was shaking his head in bewilderment as he headed back to his office and closed the linking door behind him.

It was quite some time before Dexter Hankin stopped ranting, accusing the marshal of being some kind of idiot for thinking that he would come back to Claymore if he'd raped a girl here.

'Of course I've been here before,'

Dexter roared back, in answer to Ben's question and followed it up with a question of his own. 'Tell me who hasn't since they allowed the saloon girls to operate? I remember Todd telling me that he'd been here with you and that you liked the place. He said something about you getting into a fight with some feller who knew you from way back who had a score to settle because you'd killed his brother.'

'What else did Todd tell you about me?'

'Just some things about your past and why you didn't carry a pistol. You must have raped that girl, because I sure as hell didn't.'

Ben was thinking about Suzanne recognizing him and he was remembering some of the confused thoughts he'd been having. If only he could recall what happened while he was here, but maybe if he did he would uncover something that he was ashamed of. Everything seemed so crazy and now he and Dexter Hankin might end up dangling from a rope. He didn't like Dexter very much, but despite his reputation with women he didn't think Dexter had raped Josie Webster, but maybe he didn't know Dexter well enough to make a judgement.

11

Ben had been awake for some time, wondering what to make of yesterday's events and thinking about Madeline and Milton Hankin. What would they be feeling when they heard that Dexter wouldn't be coming home? Ben had been thinking back to the times when Dexter had been groping the saloon girls, ignoring their protests, and Ben wasn't as sure about his innocence as he was yesterday. Dexter could afford any saloon girl he wanted so why would he need do such a thing to a young girl? But Josie hadn't hesitated in identifying him as her attacker.

Tuke arrived with a regulation ration of beans and bread, but it was destined for Dexter and not Ben.

'You ain't getting fed here today,' he growled at Ben.

Ben heard Tuke tell Dexter what he'd

done to his breakfast to add some extra spice to it. Either Dexter wasn't hungry, or he didn't have the stomach for it because when Tuke passed by Ben's cell he was carrying the plate containing the untouched food.

Tuke was in an ugly mood when he returned a few minutes later and opened Ben's cell and told him that the marshal wanted to speak to him.

Marshal Slaney looked troubled as he gestured for Ben to sit down and have some coffee.

'I've spent a lot of time thinking this thing over and I still don't know what's going on. I've been asking myself if either you or that Hankin feller did anything to Josie then why would you risk coming back? I don't know if you killed Todd Hankin, like his brother claims you did, but what I think doesn't really matter. The killing took place outside my jurisdiction and I haven't received any formal request from the marshal in Tremaine Creek to detain you if you turned up here. So, I'm going to turn you loose.'

Ben was surprised by the marshal's words and said, 'I swear on my ma's memory that I didn't kill him, Marshal.' Ben didn't have any memory of his ma, but it was the only thing he could think of to express his innocence to the marshal.

Tuke just shook his head and looked at the marshal in a way that made it clear that he did not share the marshal's view.

'What's going to happen to Dexter Hankin, Marshal? His pa's a wealthy rancher and Dexter could pay for a saloon girl every night of the week, so I just don't see him doing that thing with the girl. He's got a sister about Josie's age and I'm sure there's been some kind of mistake.'

The marshal looked troubled again, but said that it would be up to a jury to decide. He warned Ben that not all folks would have heard the word about Hankin's arrest and there might still be some hostility towards him. Then he revealed some news that came as a shock to Ben.

'You ought to know that Josie's uncle, Caleb Webster, hasn't been seen these past few weeks. Hankin told me that you claim to have seen his brother's killer ride off, but couldn't describe him. If I was a betting man I would say that Webster could be Todd Hankin's killer. He might have found out that you worked on the Hankin ranch and killed the wrong man by mistake and now he's gone to ground somewhere.'

Ben asked if he could talk to Dexter and explained that he wanted to send a wire to Dexter's pa so that he could get him some kind of legal representation. The marshal told Tuke to shut up after he'd said that some folks might save everyone the trouble of a trial.

'There'll be no lynching while I'm marshal,' declared Slaney, and then added, 'If anyone is stupid enough to try and take the law into their own hands then they'll feel the blast from one of those.' He nodded his head in the direction of the case on the wall that contained a fine collection of rifles and shotguns. Tuke looked annoyed when the marshal told Ben that it was OK for him to talk to the prisoner. The word prisoner had Ben thinking that was a description that fitted him until a short while ago. But he didn't get the response he expected when he told Dexter Hankin that he wanted to help him now that he was free.

'I don't want any help from you, Oakes,' Dexter snapped and then his voice became agitated. 'I don't understand why that dumb marshal didn't keep you locked up until Marshal Parrin came and took you back to Tremaine Creek.'

'Please yourself, but you're in big trouble, Dexter. I'm only offering to help you for Madeline's sake. She believes me about Todd and I don't know why you can't. You know that me and Todd were close, even closer than you and him were.'

Ben turned and started to walk away from the cells.

'Wait,' shouted Dexter, his voice sounding desperate now. 'Maybe it might be best if you send a telegraph message to my pa. He'll know what to do to get me out of here.'

'Whatever he decides to do, I hope it's legal,' Ben said, and then added a warning, 'because that marshal won't be pushed around and he'll kill anyone who tries to set you free.'

Ben left the marshal's office and headed straight for the telegraph office that was attached to the railroad station. The elderly feller looked as though he might be close to retirement and he didn't rush himself as he jotted down the details from Ben, but in the end, he was really helpful. Ben was thinking that old man Hankin was in for one hell of a surprise when he realized who had sent the telegram asking for urgent help for his son. The telegraph man told Ben that he wasn't certain what sort of operation they had at the Tremaine Creek telegraph office but he could check back later to see if there was any reply. Ben told him he would call back in the morning.

Ben headed back into the town. He was looking forward to a few beers, but decided to book himself a bed at a hotel before he visited the saloon. His visit to the Merton Hotel didn't go as expected. The sneaky-looking fellow told him that they were full and he should try the Park Hotel, situated at the end of Main Street. He said it catered for working men. Ben would have bet that the Merton Hotel wasn't fully booked and he gave the hotel manager a mean look until he could see his discomfort and then said, 'Thanks for nothing, you little runt.'

Ben reached the saloon on his way to the other hotel and discovered that his thirst for a beer was more desperate than he'd thought, so he climbed the steps to the Salt Box Saloon. He was certain that his visit there wouldn't be as eventful as the one he'd experienced in the other saloon yesterday where he'd met Suzanne. Ben had never seen such an impressive saloon door as the Salt Box with its ornate-patterned, gold-coloured scroll work. He wondered if it had once belonged to an ancient church. When he stepped inside, he paused to take in the splendour of the interior. He'd seen fancy fittings before and giant chandeliers, but not as grand as these. There were two bars and he made his way towards the long one straight ahead. The place was crowded which made him feel comfortable, because he didn't get too much attention. He'd noted that there were more men dressed in what he called Sunday best clothes, rather than his own attire. The barman greeted him with. 'Howdy stranger,' which pleased Ben, because that's what he wanted to be in this town, a stranger. He ordered his beer and while it was being served he scanned the saloon again. It had three card tables and a piano that was raised three feet off the ground. Ben smiled when he saw the old timer who was playing and wondered how he managed to climb the small ladder to reach it.

Ben was sipping his fourth beer and thinking perhaps he would head for the hotel after this one, when a fellow dressed like a man he'd once seen in the circus, gave a blast on a trumpet. It was meant to grab everyone's attention, but it didn't and most folks carried on with their chin wagging. Even the piano player continued playing until circus man roared out his name, which was Ludwig, and told him to stop. It was a strange name to Ben, but there were plenty of those in a country that seemed to attract folks from just about everywhere.

'Gentlemen, it's what you've all been waiting for,' circus man boomed out. His voice had more success than his trumpet and he continued to an almost silent audience. 'It's almost dance time, so you'll be needing to fill your glasses if you don't want to miss any of the girls' performance. Some of you know what's coming, but for those visiting for the first time, be prepared to see a sight that will have you drooling.'

'Stop your yapping, Hugo, and bring on those beauties,' someone seated close to the stage shouted.

'Patience, mister,' Hugo replied to the heckler.

'Yeah, bring them on, you great, fat blabbermouth,' echoed a drunken cowboy who had reached for the handle of his pistol, intending to use it to make Hugo get on with the proceedings. The man's hand was gripped from behind and he felt the barrel of a pistol pressed against his neck.

'You're leaving, mister. Now move out and don't make a fuss,' the huge security man growled.

Two minutes later the man was hurled outside onto the dusty street. He was either too drunk to remember, or didn't know that the owners of the Salt Box employed security men to keep

things under control. They had oper-
ated in the saloon since the town
council had threatened to close the
place down following the deaths of
three men in a brawl.

'Now we've said goodnight to the
troublemaker, let's get on with the
show,' Hugo continued, obviously used
to such an interruption and unruffled
by it.

The curtains were drawn back and
four stunning girls raced onto the stage
and took a bow. The girls smiled and
their eyes showed their excitement as
they received a tumultuous welcome
from most of those gathered through-
out all parts of the saloon. Some men
stood up and others climbed onto
chairs to get a better look, but stepped
down again when they received threats
from those whose view had been
blocked.

'Introducing for your delight, we
have, Melanie, Teresa, Myra and the
lovely Linda.'

The girls stepped forward as their

names were called out and waved towards the whistling and hooting cowboys who had gathered in front of the stage and were ogling the shapely forms in front of them. The girls were all wearing white Stetsons, red skirts with tassels attached and blue blouses that were cut low to show off their ample bosoms. Ben decided that Linda had the prettiest face and a natural smile, unlike the other girls who had forced smiles and showed too much of their teeth. Myra was no dancer, but she was the one who got the biggest cheer when the girls did a solo spot, because she knew how to wiggle her body in a way that had some of the men going crazy.

By the time the girls stopped for a short interval, Ben was beginning to feel the effects of the beer. Perhaps it was the relief of being out of jail and free, at least for the moment, that made him want to enjoy himself tonight.

'Gentlemen, we are going to try a new idea tonight,' Hugo announced.

'The girls will be passing amongst you selling raffle tickets at a dollar each. Remember to keep your hands to yourselves and show the girls some respect. Now, the winner of the raffle will be invited to choose which girl he would like to spend a little time with. By *time with* I don't mean they'll be discussing the history of dance, or the rivers, lakes and mountains of our great country. So, get your money out and you might be in for a night that you will never forget.'

There was a lot of hollering and dollar bills being waved in the air as the girls came down the steps of the small stage and peeled off to different parts of the saloon. Ben was bemused by the eagerness of some cowboys to part with their money, especially those who would be in no fit state to enjoy the prize should they have the winning ticket.

'Would you like a ticket, handsome?' the sweet voice said, addressing Ben. He turned and was about to decline politely, until he saw that it was Linda. The beautiful smile that he'd seen from a distance was even better close up as he saw her pale-blue eyes and lovely skin. Ben reached into his pocket and then handed over his money and told her he wanted two tickets.

Linda handed him the green-coloured tickets, winked and said, 'I hope you win.'

Ben was thinking that she said that to everyone, but she didn't.

When Hugo told the girls to return to the stage and resume their dancing, he said that tickets could still be bought from the barman until the draw was made in about half-an-hour's time. Ben suddenly felt tired and wondered if he wanted to stay much longer, then he spotted Deputy Tuke who was glowering at him. He didn't know how long he'd been there, but Ben wasn't going to let the miserable son of a bitch spoil his enjoyment. Ben stared back at him until Tuke turned away and started talking to the man next to him at the bar.

The barman offered Ben a refill, but he declined just as Hugo announced that it was the moment everyone had been waiting for. He invited a cowboy near the stage to come up and pick a number from the small mountain of tickets that were in a large, wide-brimmed Stetson.

'You'd better not pick out your own ticket, cowboy,' someone shouted.

Ludwig played a short burst of music and Hugo asked the man to make the draw. The cowboy grinned as he pulled out a ticket which was taken from him by Hugo.

'The winning number is on a yellow ticket and it's number . . . ' Hugo paused and looked embarrassed before he said, 'Sorry folks, but this ticket is blank. It must have been at the beginning of the book, or it's a misprint.'

There were lots of groans from various parts of the saloon, mostly from those who had been holding yellow tickets and others who had thrown their tickets away because they weren't yellow.

The cowboy was invited to draw another ticket and this time it was green.

'And the lucky ticket is green and number twenty-two,' Hugo announced.

There were cries of 'fix' and some asking for their money back. Others scrambled on the floor looking for their discarded green tickets.

'Will the lucky man step forward, or is he too shy?' Hugo called out and followed it with, 'Come on, someone must have it.'

Ben's thoughts were faraway when the man next to him pointed to Ben's ticket on the bar and shouted out in an excited voice, 'Hey, buddy, you've won.'

'Over here. He's won,' the man shouted again.

'Give a big hand for the winner,' called out Hugo, who started clapping and invited the winner to come up on stage.

Ben received much back slapping and advice on which girl he should pick as he made his way through the crowd and on to the stage.

'Myra, Myra,' was the chant that was heard above the others. Myra was certainly the most well endowed of the girls and she took a bow and blew a kiss to her admirers. Hugo shook Ben's hand and then took the ticket from him and then shouted out,

'Hold on, this is twenty-three, not twenty-two.' Hugo laughed, then quickly announced that he was only joking.

'So, cowboy, what's your name?'

'His name's Ben Oakes and he's a rapist,' Tuke shouted out.

'It sounds like someone's a poor loser out there, Ben,' said Hugo and then continued, 'Are you going to choose the popular and lovely Myra, or do you think one of the other girls will best give you a night to remember? Name the girl.'

'They're all lovely, but it has to be Linda.' Ben replied awkwardly.

There was more hollering from the crowd and then they began chanting. 'Linda, Linda.'

Linda was beckoned forward by Hugo. She smiled at Ben and her face coloured as she blushed a little. The other girls seemed happy enough, except Myra who looked as though she'd just swallowed some sour cream.

'What happens now?' Ben whispered, as he and Linda walked off the stage and into the bar area to loud applause and some crude advice.

'I think we're supposed to go upstairs,' Linda replied.

Ben would have been as embarrassed as hell if he hadn't consumed so much beer, but right now he was actually enjoying the occasion. They were almost at the foot of the stairs when Tuke appeared behind them.

'You must be some special sort of slut to go with a rapist,' Tuke called out.

Linda was shocked by his hostility and tried to hurry away, but Tuke reached out to pull her back. Ben let go of Linda's hand and rammed his fist hard into Tuke's belly and then delivered a head butt as Tuke bent forward as a result of the first blow to his body. Tuke cried out in pain as he fell to the floor, his nose dripping blood that was soon smeared across his shirt. Ben hovered over the fallen lawman waiting and hoping he would get up so he could inflict more pain on the man who had displayed a cruel streak during Ben's stay in the cell across the street.

Tuke staggered to his feet, but he was in no state to fight. He wiped the blood from his face with the back of his hand and he waved away the security man who had appeared.

'I'll get you for this, Oakes, and I won't be wearing a badge,' snarled Tuke and weaved his way towards the door.

Ben and Linda continued their way up the stairs and were soon in a large room that had a fancy chandelier hanging from the centre of the ceiling and an assortment of pictures on the walls. The room was dominated by a large bed that had elaborate brass posts at each corner and purple silk sheets.

'Would you like a drink, Ben? Your name is Ben, isn't it?' Linda queried.

'I think I've had enough to drink,' Ben replied, and then added, 'My name is Ben, but I'm no rapist like that deputy said.'

'I'm sure you're not, but why does he think you are?'

'It's a long story and if you don't mind I'd rather we didn't talk about it. I don't want to offend you, but I think I'd better leave.'

Linda had already started to unbutton her blouse and when she lay back on the bed he realized that he'd made a good choice: Linda didn't just have a pretty face. He sat on the edge of the bed and gave a sigh and said, 'I can't do this.'

Linda sat up. She looked surprised and then sullen as she lowered her eyelashes.

'I thought you liked me. Is it because you've got a sweetheart, or maybe a wife? Is that what's bothering you, or perhaps you're wishing you'd picked Myra?'

'I picked you because you were the prettiest girl on the stage.'

'You're not making sense, Ben. You say you like me so why aren't we making love right now instead of you keeping your distance? Don't you even like these?' Linda asked as she cupped her large breasts.

'I could never go with a saloon girl, Linda. It's nothing personal, it's just the way I am. I've been tempted a few times and I am now, but I know I'd regret it.'

Linda looked concerned for a moment and asked if he had some sort of medical problem, or was he frightened of catching some disease off her. She reassured him that he need have no worries on that score with her, or any of the other girls.

Ben smiled and said, 'I wasn't thinking about anything like that. I have an idea that you haven't been doing this job for long.'

'I've only ever been with one man and he was my husband. He died last year when he was trampled by stampeding cattle while he was working on the range near where we'd settled. I joined these girls a few weeks ago because I've always wanted to dance on the stage. But, don't get me wrong, I knew there were other things I was expected to do, like now.'

'Linda, it's nothing personal,' Ben said, trying to reassure her.

'Maybe you have some kind of religious reason because you were brought up in a Bible punching family,' said Linda whose frustration was turning to anger.

Ben smiled again before he said, 'I was brought up by saloon girls ever since my ma abandoned me when I was six weeks old. That's why I could never sleep with one of you girls. I just know I couldn't. It would be like sleeping with my sister.'

Linda's eyes filled with tears, 'That's the sweetest thing I've ever heard, honey. Why didn't you tell me that right away and then I wouldn't have quizzed you like I did? Come here and give this sister a big hug.'

Ben felt relieved that she'd accepted his reasons, but as she pressed her firm body against his he wondered if he would regret what he had just turned down.

They decided that in order to save Linda's reputation it would be best if Ben stayed in the room until the following morning. He lay at the opposite end of the bed to Linda and he struggled to get to sleep, mainly on account of Linda's sighing and moaning in her sleep.

★　★　★

Ben had dressed quietly so he wouldn't disturb the sleeping Linda. He'd been awake since sun-up and been admiring her beauty. He paused to take a final look before he prepared to tiptoe out of the room. She had discarded the bed covers and he could see her completely naked body. He knew that if he saw Linda again before he left Claymore then he would likely succumb to her beauty and forget about his principle of not sleeping with a saloon girl. He had a feeling that he would often think about the night he turned down a prize that some men would have died for.

12

Milton Hankin drummed his fingers on his desk and studied the man he had ordered to come here. Hankin had forgiven Madeline for helping Oakes escape, but he had been brooding since he'd sent Dexter to find Todd's killer. His useless, good-for-nothing son just wasn't up to it. Oh, he could talk tough and make promises, but he had no backbone. Milton wished it was different and he wanted to give his son the opportunity to prove himself, but not if it meant giving Ben Oakes the chance to escape being caught and made to pay for what he'd done. He needed to take out some insurance in case he was right about his son fouling up and Oakes headed for Mexico or some other faraway place. Now he hoped this man would end his torment, even though he didn't like him. Ewen Macey was as slippery as an eel, but he was loyal and that was important.

When he'd finished explaining to Macey what he wanted him to do, he asked, 'Do you think you can handle him? I don't want the law involved. I just want you to kill him and bring me back some proof that he's dead.'

Macey looked uneasy. 'You want me to bring his body back here. Is that what you mean, Mr Hankin?'

Hankin's face reddened with irritation. 'No, I don't want his body brought back and I don't want his death linked to me or my family. Is that clear?'

Macey acknowledged that his orders were clear and that he would make sure that the family name would not be involved in any way, but he was still puzzled about how he could prove that Oakes was dead. But then Milton explained.

'I saw Oakes stripped off once while he was doing some work in the barn. He's got a large, ugly birthmark on his shoulder. It must be two inches long and almost as wide. I've heard some folks say that such a thing is the mark of the Devil and I'm thinking that it might be true. Anyway, you can cut it out and bring it back here. Then you can have your reward and you won't be disappointed.'

Macey had reached the door when Milton Hankin called after him, 'Oh, and Macey, when you get to Claymore Ridge make sure that Dexter doesn't see you. He mustn't realize that you are after Oakes. Try and arrange for Oakes to have a slow death. You might get the chance to show him the little memento that you will be bringing back to me.'

Macey left the study thinking that Milton Hankin was one sick, evil-minded son of a bitch, but he still admired him. He was going to do exactly what he'd been told, but he might throw in a few extras of his own. But he didn't intend getting too close to Ben Oakes, unless he was already dying or dead. Macey knew all about

Ben Oakes, or whatever name he chose to use, and he wasn't about to confront him face to face.

★ ★ ★

Macey had been gone for less than a couple of hours when Doug Hington, the Hankin foreman, was standing in Milton Hankin's study. Next to him was Maribel, the Mexican maid.

'I'm too busy to be bothered with domestic problems,' Hankin snapped. 'Can't Mrs Sorrenson handle whatever problem you've got with this girl?'

'This is about your son, Mr Hankin, and I thought you'd want to hear it from Maribel.'

'If she's got herself pregnant by one of the cowhands and come here trying to pass it off as Dexter's child then she'll be looking for a new job. I wasn't born yesterday.'

'It's nothing like that, Mr Hankin, and I mean Todd, not Dexter.' Hington turned to Maribel. 'Tell Mr Hankin what you told me, Maribel. Just take your time.'

'I saw . . . ' Maribel started to say in a quiet voice and then stopped, frightened by Hankin who seemed to be angry with her. She was thinking that she should have kept what she saw to herself, even though it would have been wrong.

'Come on, girl. What did you see?' Hankin snapped, his face flushed with irritation and the effects of the whiskey he'd been consuming since breakfast.

Maribel swallowed hard and tried again, but got no further than the last time.

'For God's sake, Hington, what did this stupid girl see?'

Doug Hington gave Maribel a sympathetic look and then turned to Hankin. 'She said that on the day Todd was killed she was hanging out some washing when she saw a rider galloping away shortly after she'd heard a shot. She couldn't describe him, but I think she's telling the truth, because she isn't the sort to make things up and put herself though this. You can see what an ordeal it is for her.'

'You swear that this is true?' Hankin growled at her.

Maribel fingered her rosary beads, looked Hankin in the eye and said, 'I swear on my brother and sister's lives that what I told Señor Hington is true.'

Hankin took another gulp of whiskey while he studied the girl and then told Hington to tell her to wait outside because he had some matters to discuss with him.

Hington led Maribel to the door and returned to face Hankin who was refilling his large whiskey glass to the brim. He'd never seen Hankin so obviously drunk before, or with sweat on his upper lip.

'Right,' said Hankin in his usual businesslike manner, 'I want you tell Mrs Sorrenson to pay the girl off with a generous sum. Apparently she's been a bit slack lately and Dexter's been complaining about her. She's obviously upset about what she saw and it's probably best for her if she's not around here to be reminded of it. Get one of the hands to take her into town in the buggy and book her into a hotel until she can find another job. Tell the hotel to send me her bill.'

Doug Hington was about to mention that perhaps the marshal should be told when Milton Hankin threatened him with a warning. If he found out that Hington or the girl blabbed about what she'd seen he would make sure that Hington never worked for anyone in the State of Arizona. But Hington had something that had been preying on his mind and now was the time to get it off his chest.

'Mr Hankin, I guess Dexter was just too upset to attend his brother's funeral.'

Hankin's face showed his irritation once more. 'How could he when he wasn't here?'

'But he came by my place on the morning that Todd was killed. I saw

166

him riding away when I went home after finishing work early that day. My wife said that he'd called to see me, but he didn't tell her what it was about. I remember because she had been crying. The silly woman was upset because a critter had killed some of her chickens.'

'So where the hell did he go? Because he sure as hell didn't come home. Anyway, it doesn't matter now. Nothing much matters now,' said Hankin and waved his hand to dismiss his foreman.

Hankin waited for Hington to leave and then gulped the whiskey until the glass was once again empty. He held his head in his hands and sighed heavily. The knock on the door startled him and he bellowed an invitation to enter. He was expecting it to be Hington again, but it was Wendell Collyer, the Hankin attorney. Collyer was a serious-faced man, with cold brown eyes and a head that had just a few thin straggly remains of what had once been thick black hair. He wore gold-rimmed spectacles and, as always, was immaculately dressed in an expensive black suit.

'Collyer, I wasn't expecting you. Do we have an appointment?'

'No, sir, but we do have one for next Thursday morning to finalize the purchase of some investment stock that was recommended to you. I'm afraid I'm here on personal and urgent business.'

'What do you mean by personal?' Hankin quizzed, and started filling his glass with whiskey.

Collyer had taken some papers from his black leather document case. He cleared his throat and said. 'Your son Dexter is in serious trouble. You've had a telegram from Claymore Ridge and it seems that he's been accused of raping a young woman.'

Hankin was thinking that at least his lazy good for nothing son had got as far as Claymore, even though it was a waste of time in the light of what the Mexican girl had revealed.

Hankin was lost in his thoughts

about Todd's killing and his orders to Dexter, and then there was Macey. He had ordered an innocent man to be killed. What a mess!

'I know it must be distressing for you,' said Collyer, wondering if he was going to get much sense out of the drunken and confused Hankin.

'I suppose he wants me to arrange to send him some money so he can pay off the little trollop. Is that it? Or maybe there is no girl and he just wants to trick me into sending him money?'

'Your son didn't send the wire.'

'Then who did?' barked Hankin, his eyes wild as he glowered at Collyer.

'Well, this might come as a shock to you,' said Collyer, trying to prepare him and wondering what he would make of it in his present state of mind. 'It was Ben Oakes. Dexter is in jail awaiting trial.'

'Oakes!' Hankin cried out in disbelief. 'How is Oakes involved in this and why isn't he in jail?' Hankin was confused and forgetting that he now knew that Oakes was innocent.

'I don't know what's happening back there in Claymore Ridge, except that your son is in serious trouble and it appears that Oakes is trying to help him.'

Hankin was thinking about the mess again and cursing his son for bringing more trouble to the family, but at least there was an easy solution to this problem.

'Send whatever money they need to give to the girl and her family. Handle it like you did the other times.'

'Mr Hankin, this isn't like the other times. Your son is in jail and proceedings for his trial are under way. We need to arrange for him to get some legal representation. That's the only way you can help him and it needs to be done urgently. I should warn you that it is not uncommon for men to be hanged for rape in some parts of the state, including Claymore Ridge.'

'Damn, that useless, good-for-nothing son of mine. I've a good mind to let him face the consequences.' Hankin roared, and then calmed himself and added, 'I need to think about this.'

Collyer waited to give Hankin time to deliberate, but the man seemed lost in his thoughts and clearly in some distress.

'Sometimes these things are not as bad as they seem,' said Collyer trying to comfort his most valuable client. 'Dexter might be totally innocent, but I need to remind you, sir, that we haven't got much time. I know a very good man who specializes in these sort of cases. His name is Robert Lawrence. I could instruct him to represent Dexter if you want me to.'

Hankin pondered some more and then said, 'Go ahead and get this feller. Do whatever it takes. Oh, and Collyer, while you're here, are you absolutely certain that my new will that you drew up last week is absolutely watertight? I don't want some smart lawyer picking holes in it when the time comes.'

'Your will is quite straightforward, sir. There will be just the one beneficiary in accordance with your wishes and that is your daughter, Madeline.'

'Good; then I expect you'll want to get on with this Dexter business. It doesn't matter what it costs. Just make sure he gets off and the Hankin name isn't tarnished. And don't forget about that other thing I told you about in strict confidence.'

'I won't forget and I'll do whatever I can should the need arise,' Collyer replied, as he gathered up his papers and wished his client a good day.

Hankin had already drained the remaining whiskey from the bottle before Collyer had closed the door behind him and then gulped back the contents of the glass. He looked towards the cabinet that held a fresh supply of whiskey, undecided whether to go and get it. He started to get out of his chair and then slumped back. He muttered to himself and then picked up the family photograph from his desk. It was taken when Todd and Dexter were young boys and Madeline was just a baby being held in her mother's arms. Dear Elizabeth, at least she had been spared the tragedy that had befallen the family and the shame that was to come. The plans he'd dreamed of lay in ruins. His sons would never inherit the empire that he'd built for them. They had been his driving motivation and all that he'd worked for meant nothing now. He wondered how long it would take Macey to find Oakes and shoot him in the back. He thought of sending someone after Macey and trying to stop him. Perhaps he could get a warning to Oakes, but that would mean admitting that he'd arranged to kill an innocent man. For the first time in his life he felt helpless and confused,

Wendell Collyer was still on Hankin land but too far away to hear either the shot that had ended Milton Hankin's life, or Mrs Sorrenson's screams when she found Hankin slumped over his desk. There was a gun in his hand and the note he'd written was smeared with his blood. It read:

My Dear Daughter Madeline
I am very proud of you.

I have learned that Ben Oakes did not kill your brother, but now I fear that he may be dead before his innocence is known because I have sent someone to kill him.

Please forgive my weakness, but I have grown tired of life.

Your Loving Daddy

PS Ewen Macey is loyal and will uphold the good name of the Hankin family and protect you from dangers and interference from your brother Dexter, but you must never marry him.

Wendel Collyer would be returning to the ranch sooner than expected to sort out the legal details of Milton Hankin's sad end. Now he was the only living person who knew of the secret that Milton Hankin had lived with for so many years.

13

Madeline had been asleep for over an hour on the last part of the railroad journey to Claymore Ridge and she was drowsy when Wendel Collyer shook her gently.

'We're here, Miss Hankin,' the family lawyer said, in his usual quiet, calm voice. Madeline couldn't have made the journey to attend her brother's trial without him. She'd got to know him quite well since her father had died as he'd explained the significance of her father's will. She'd told him that she wanted her brother Dexter to have an equal share of everything, but he'd cautioned her and reminded her that she would be going against her father's wishes if she did that.

Collyer insisted on carrying Madeline's small travel bag as they left the train and made their way down the platform. The train had been almost empty and they were the only passengers leaving the train at Claymore Ridge, with the rest destined for Torres which was the last stop on this stretch of the railroad. Collyer had explained that Robert Lawrence who was representing Dexter would probably be there to meet them, but he wasn't. Collyer left Madeline and approached the uniformed man near the ticket office. He returned and told Madeline that they would have to wait a few minutes while the luggage was loaded onto a buggy that was outside the station and it would take them to the hotel.

★ ★ ★

Madeline had been back East on several visits when she was younger and stayed with relatives, so staying in a hotel was going to be a new experience for her. Collyer had arranged everything and she was impressed by the size and comfort of her room at the Merton hotel.

The one thing that Collyer couldn't help her with was the whereabouts of Ewen Macey who hadn't been seen since the day her father died. No one at the ranch knew where he might have gone, but Doug Hington, the ranch foreman, told her Macey had been moody and restless in recent weeks and must have moved on. She had always liked Ewen Macey and hoped he would return, because she had a feeling that Ben might not want to work on the Hankin Ranch after the way he'd been treated following Todd's death. She would need a lot of help to run the ranch and she had remembered her daddy's praise for Ewen, but also his warning about not marrying him. She'd always valued her daddy's advice, but she would make her own mind up about whom she would marry one day and be ruled by her heart and nothing else.

Madeline was no longer the wide-eyed young woman who had been rarely seen without a smile on her face. Life had delivered her too many blows for them not to have taken their toll. She told Collyer that she didn't want to dine, preferring to go and visit her brother, but he'd persuaded her to rest for a while and have some dinner before visiting Dexter. She took his advice, although she didn't rest, anxious to know how her brother had coped with being locked away and facing such uncertainty. But her thoughts also turned to Ben, wondering if he was still here in Claymore and she was anxious to know if Collyer's telegraph telling him he wasn't a wanted man any more had reached him. After her father's funeral, Doug Hington had told her about the maid seeing a rider on the day of Todd's death, but Madeline hadn't revealed that Ben might have been killed on her daddy's orders.

★　★　★

Wendel Collyer watched Madeline pick at her meal as they sat in the lavish dining-room of the hotel. Her spirits had lifted earlier when he told her that he had spoken to Oakes who had received the telegraph and was aware of the maid's statement and knew that he was no longer wanted for Todd's murder. Collyer said it wouldn't be a good idea for Madeline to speak to Oakes until the trial was over.

Wendel Collyer hoped that he hadn't made a big mistake when he trusted his judgement and betrayed his client's confidentiality and told Oakes about a secret concerning the late Milton Hankin.

When the smartly dressed man approached them as they were leaving the hotel Madeline had already guessed that it was Robert Lawrence before the introductions were made. Robert Lawrence oozed charm and confidence and she was pleased that this man would be the one that might save her brother's life.

'What a nice man,' said Madeline, as they parted and crossed Main Street heading for the marshal's office.

'He has a very good reputation,' replied Wendel Collyer diplomatically, thinking that Lawrence might lay claim to many things, but being a nice man was not one of them. But if Dexter Hankin ended up being grateful to Lawrence then it would probably be because he was actually a ruthless swine and a liar. He was a man who would do anything to win a case for his client, even if he knew they were guilty of a despicable crime.

Madeline spent less than twenty minutes with her brother. They discussed their father's death, but she didn't mention her father's will even when Dexter had said that he had plans for the ranch if things went well for him tomorrow. He told her that he'd spent many hours talking over his case with Robert Lawrence who was confident Dexter would be able to leave Claymore tomorrow with his name having being cleared. Madeline did her best to offer her support, but by the time she left her brother she wasn't convinced about his innocence. He'd admitted being in Claymore about the time of the rape, but he couldn't be clear about the actual time. Dexter had always had an eye for the ladies and Madeline had heard rumours that their daddy had got Dexter out of trouble with a number of them. Madeline had remembered seeing a girl from the town call at the ranch a few years ago with a young child. Madeline had been looking out of the window at the time and saw her daddy and Dexter talking to her and a man who must have been her pa. Madeline had been puzzled why her daddy had handed the girl's pa some money before they rode off in a small buggy. When Madeline became more worldly wise she knew that the payment had been to get rid of them.

Wendel Collyer was waiting for Madeline when she came out of the marshal's office, but she declined his offer to escort her back to the hotel before he went for an evening stroll. She was thinking that it must be fate when she saw Ben leaving the general store. When he approached her she looked in the direction of Wendel Collyer who was some distance away. She recalled his warning that she shouldn't meet with Ben until after the trial.

Ben smiled and she quickly dismissed any idea of following Collyer's advice.

Ben touched the brim of his Stetson and his face became sombre. 'I was sorry to hear about your pa, Madeline. He'd always been good to me and it was true what folks said about him treating me like a son. He'd spent some time in places that I grew up in and we used to talk about those.'

Madeline's eyes misted up. 'It has been like a long nightmare. First, it was Todd's death, and then poor Daddy. Now there's this business hanging over Dexter. I don't know what I'm going to do after tomorrow, Ben.'

'You'll be able to handle it, Madeline, because you're a gutsy girl. You believed in me and now you must believe in Dexter.'

Ben was hoping his words would bring her comfort, but she still looked full of anguish and he wasn't ready for her response when it came.

'Ben, you must be careful because you could still be in danger. Daddy was confused after Todd's death and he sent someone to kill you before he found out that you were innocent. I think that was one of the reasons why he took his own life.'

Ben wasn't surprised to hear that Milton had sent someone after him. He tried to ease her anxiety by explaining that whoever it was must have heard about his innocence and abandoned his mission. Ben was about to receive another surprise.

'Ben, will you come back to the ranch and work for me?' she asked. Her tone was desperate.

'I'm not sure that would be a good

idea, Madeline. I never got on with Dexter like I did with Todd. I don't think your brother would be too pleased to see me back.'

'What Dexter thinks doesn't really matter, Ben,' she snapped back, showing a hardness he hadn't seen before, but then her tone softened when she added, 'I want you to, but if you have other ideas then I'll need to get someone else.'

She looked disappointed when he told her he couldn't return to the Hankin ranch until he'd tracked down Josie Webster's Uncle Caleb. Ben confessed to Madeline about Todd's dying word being Claymore and that it was possible that Josie's rape and Todd's killing were linked and Caleb might be the killer.

Her face showed her relief when Ben said, 'I'll stay here for three weeks to see if he shows up, or I find out where he might be holed up, and then I'll head back to your ranch and do all I can to help you.' Her eyes became misty and she hugged him as she thanked him. He held her close knowing that it was what they both wanted, but they pulled apart realizing that this wasn't the right time or place. Ben walked her to the hotel and they hugged again as he bid her goodnight and said that he hoped to see her again after the trial. The man sitting on a sidewalk bench opposite them had his Stetson partly covering his face and had been pretending to be dozing, but he had been watching them. He intended to kill Ben Oakes, but he would bide his time.

★ ★ ★

Madeline couldn't sleep, plagued by her thoughts. She scolded herself for being selfish and thinking of her love for Ben at a time when her family had recently suffered tragedy. This time tomorrow she might be facing more grief if Robert Lawrence's confidence was misplaced and her brother was found guilty. She'd always liked Ben, but now she knew that she loved him because she couldn't rid him from her thoughts. She felt that strange sensation again which seemed to occur when she was thinking of Ben. She felt her face flushing as she imagined Ben lying beside her and touching her in places that until now only she had explored and felt such pleasure from. She wanted him in a way that made her shameful, but she didn't want to stop thinking these thoughts that brought her a new and even more pleasurable feeling. She gave a long moan and relaxed before drifting into a blissful sleep.

14

Judge Jerome Linus Spellinger called the court to order. He was seventy-two years old with no distinguishing features except maybe his long beard that was snow-white. He was calm and assured as he explained the procedures to the jury and the legal representatives. He singled out Robert Lawrence, Dexter's defence attorney for a special warning. 'Mr Lawrence, I will not tolerate any attempt to intimidate witnesses with threats about perjury. I am well aware of your style and I do not approve of it.'

Robert Lawrence gave a polite acknowledgement, but he was confident that he could conduct Dexter Hankin's defence without being hampered by a judge who had a reputation for protecting witnesses from hostile questioning.

Robert Lawrence had been on God's earth for thirty-three years, but folks would have thought it had been much longer. He was tall and lean with cold eyes and his mouth was usually set in a firm expression as though in deep concentration. His pale-blue eyes appeared penetrating even when he smiled, which was rare, unless he was smirking at or charming someone. His brooding looks seemed to attract women, but he had rebuffed many attempts by would-be matchmakers. There was only room for one love in his world and that was his work. He came from a long line of legal people and had three brothers in the profession. The betting money was on him to become a federal judge one day. Judge Spellinger nodded towards Jerimah Hague, the clerk of the court to signal him to call the first witness for the prosecution.

'Will Mr Ben Oakes take the stand,' Hague boomed out.

Ben had been briefed about the procedures which began with him being sworn in after which Judge Spellinger invited the prosecution lawyer, William Henry Bilson to open the case.

William Bilson was barely out of law school and came from a family of poor farmers in Southern Nevada. His uncle Edgar had encouraged him to take up the law and given him financial support. He was twenty-five years old, with a boyish face and thick, blond, curly hair. This was the first time he'd prosecuted in a case of rape, but he was determined to do his best and make sure that the defendant paid a hefty price for such a despicable deed.

'Mr Oakes, can you confirm that you were present when Miss Josie Webster identified Dexter Hankin as the man who attacked her?'

Ben acknowledged that he was and in answer to further questions said that he had never met Josie Webster and he had no idea why someone might have used his name. He was not aware of another Ben Oakes. Bilson said that he had no further questions, prompting the judge to invite the defence to question the witness. Ben usually found that his first impression of people didn't change with time and his initial view was that Robert Lawrence was a slippery snake.

Lawrence shuffled his papers, letting Ben wait for his opening question, but his ploy hadn't gone unnoticed by Judge Spellinger who shook his head and sounded weary already when he said, 'Mr Lawrence, maybe you'll prepare your case before coming to court. If you're not ready I'll order the witness to stand down until you are.'

'I'm sorry, Your Honour. I just need to check on some important matter relating to Mr Oakes's background in Jolin County, but I'm ready now.' Lawrence's apology had been delivered without a trace of embarrassment, but he now knew that the judge might well be stricter than he had hoped.

Lawrence sighed. 'Mr Oakes.' Lawrence paused and then asked, 'Does the name Sam Devine mean anything to you?'

'I guess you already know that it

does,' replied Ben, sounding a mite uninterested in the proceedings.

'According to my information, Sam Devine has killed more men than Jessie James did, but you'll know if my information is correct because your real name is Sam Devine, isn't it?'

Ben nodded in agreement, but Judge Spellinger ordered him to answer which he duly did.

'Your Honour, I will continue to address the witness as Ben Oakes to avoid any confusion. Talking of confusion, I would ask the jury to note the resemblance between Ben Oakes and Dexter Hankin.'

Bilson objected, claiming that Ben Oakes wasn't on trial. He would raise the same objection many times before Ben was asked to stand down. Judge Spellinger had sustained the objection raised when Lawrence had produced sworn testimony from Suzanne and another saloon girl that they had seen Ben in Claymore on the day Josie was raped. Lawrence didn't mind the objection because the point had already been placed in the minds of the jury and nothing the judge could say by way of directing them would change that.

'Mr Oakes, is it true that you escaped from the marshal's office in the town of Tremaine Creek whilst you were under arrest for the murder of Todd Hankin?'

Ben had answered yes before Bilson had objected to the question and pointed out that Ben was no longer a suspect following a statement by a witness that supported his client's claim that another man had ridden away from the scene of the killing. Ben's eyes were drawn in the direction of where Madeline was sitting, but she wasn't looking at him. Lawrence studied his notes again before he delivered his next question in a slow and deliberate manner.

'Mr Oakes, did you kill a man when you were just a boy of fifteen years of age?' Ben was shaken by the question. He wondered how Lawrence had found out because the killing had never been entered in any records. He was certain of that. The only person he'd ever told was Todd and he guessed Todd must have mentioned it to Dexter. Ben was tempted to deny it, but he didn't.

'Can you tell us how you came to end that man's life?'

'He was beating a woman and I stopped him. He pulled a gun on me. There was a struggle and I shot him.'

'So that's your version. Others say that it was the other way around and that you were forcing yourself on the woman, even though you were just a boy and the man tried to stop you and you shot him in cold blood. The marshal must have given you the benefit of the doubt because no charges were brought against you. Perhaps the marshal was receiving special favours from the woman who brought you up. I believe she was a notorious saloon girl who went by the name of Sandy.'

Ben felt the anger boil inside him because of the way this snake in a suit was twisting everything and insulting the woman who had been like a mother to him. He was on the point of getting out of his seat ready to shut Lawrence's foul, lying mouth when Bilson stood up and objected to the line of Lawrence's questioning. Bilson had given Ben a moment to calm down and it had stopped the court from seeing Lawrence's blood on the courtroom floor. Lawrence looked anxious because he had realized how close he'd come to being attacked by a man who had already killed before and would likely do it again. Lawrence took a moment to regain his composure before he continued his questioning, reminding himself not to mention Oakes's relationship with saloon girls again.

'But that wasn't the last time you killed a man, was it?'

'No,' replied Ben, but this time he didn't look towards Madeline, having decided not to prolong the agony of the questioning when he continued, 'I've killed four men. The last man I killed threatened to shoot me unless I drew on him so I shot him dead. I guess you already know that, so you'll know that I never faced a trial for that either. The other killings happened in a similar way and were in self-defence as well.'

'And yet you hid your past from the family who put their trust in you. If these killings were all self-defence like you claim, then why did you keep them a secret?'

'I wanted to make a new start. I never looked for trouble, but it always seemed to follow me and it isn't in my nature to walk away from it. I wanted an end to the killings. That's the reason I never carried a gun during my time at the Hankin ranch.'

'That's very commendable of you,' Lawrence said with an obvious note of sarcasm.

'Mr Lawrence,' Judge Spellinger said, with a sigh and note of impatience in his voice. 'I have been generous so far in giving you a certain amount of leeway, but now I must ask you to return to point of issue here, which is the rape of Josie Webster and not your character appraisal of the present witness.'

'Thank you, Your Honour. Your patience is appreciated,' Lawrence replied, hiding his annoyance that the judge had rumbled him.

'Mr Oakes,' he paused again and then continued, 'Mr Oakes has anyone ever said that you look like the accused, Dexter Hankin?'

'No,' Ben replied.

'I find that very hard to believe and I'm sure that anyone in this court today observing you both would have the same doubt.'

'Some folks reckoned that me and Todd Hankin could have been taken for brothers, so I suppose Dexter and me might be alike in some small way, except that he's on the skinny side compared to me and he's a fancy dresser.'

'But you could be sufficiently alike for a young girl like Josie Webster, who was under a great deal of pressure, to mistake Dexter Hankin for you. Do you think that's possible?'

Before Ben could answer Bilson objected to the question and pointed out once again that Ben wasn't on trial.

Judge Spellinger showed his irritation with Lawrence when he upheld the objection and ordered Ben to stand down.

Lawrence was about to shake his head in annoyance, but he was too controlled and experienced to risk upsetting the judge further and settled for what he'd got out of his session with Ben and he sat down.

Josie Webster was called to the stand and her voice was barely a whisper as she was sworn in. She had her head lowered when Bilson gently asked her to point out the man who had committed such a despicable offence against her person.

Dexter Hankin had sat expressionless during the proceedings so far, but he shook his head in disbelief when Josie's finger was directed at him.

197

Bilson announced that he had no further questions and Josie's face showed her relief as she started to move from the witness stand.

'I'm afraid we haven't quite finished, Miss Webster,' said Lawrence in an apologetic tone, and then added, 'I know this must be painful for you and I'll try and keep my questions brief.'

Josie relaxed a little, encouraged by the friendliness of the man whom Bilson had warned her might be accusing and cruel.

'Miss Webster, is it true that you have had a great deal of sexual experience since you were a very young girl?'

Josie was shocked by the accusation and she shook her head violently, rejecting the suggestion and then said, 'No, that's not the way I have been brought up. I'm a churchgoing girl.'

Lawrence smiled and said, 'I'm sure you are, but thankfully going to church does not prevent folks enjoying pleasures of the flesh.' His comment resulted in some mutterings and looks of disapproval from some of the ladies seated around the court.

'If only that were true,' whispered Tom Payne, dwelling on what Lawrence had said. Tom was sitting next to his prim and proper wife Mabel, whose father had always preached moderation in all things and declared that Sunday was not a day for pleasure of any kind.

'Miss Webster, according to the marshal's report you had been drinking alcohol on the day you say someone had sexual intercourse with you against your will. I find this puzzling because in my experience churchgoing young ladies do not consume alcohol and allow themselves to be picked up by complete strangers. I take it that man in question was a stranger to you.'

Josie just nodded her head in agreement, but Judge Spellinger didn't insist that she answer.

'Miss Webster, I am told that you have lived most of your life with your uncle' — Lawrence paused briefly to check his notes before continuing

— 'Caleb Webster. Would you say that your relationship with your uncle was a natural one as in the eyes of God?'

Josie became more distressed even though she didn't fully understand the question and she looked towards the judge for help.

The judge gave Lawrence a stern look while shaking his head and said, 'Mr Lawrence, please do not resort to such unwarranted innuendo.' Judge Spellinger directed the jury to ignore such attempts to undermine the reputation of the victim in this case. This time Lawrence did look mildly embarrassed. He apologized and then got Josie to confirm that her alleged attacker had told her that his name was Ben Oakes. He looked disappointed when she'd said that she couldn't remember the name of the ranch he worked on or the town nearby.

'Miss Webster, did you identify Dexter Hankin as your attacker when you saw him in the marshal's office because you thought he had been arrested?'

'I just saw him and knew it was him. I told the marshal straight away.' Lawrence pointed out that the brother of the accused had probably been killed because of mistaken identity and that she shouldn't make the same mistake and be responsible for an innocent man being sentenced to death. He also suggested that maybe she knew who the real attacker was, but had her reasons for blaming someone else. He outlined some of the reasons and she was close to tears when she denied them, but he continued to probe and hint.

'Miss Webster, do you know for certain the identity of the father of the child that you are expecting?'

'Miss Webster, you do not have to answer that question,' Judge Spellinger advised.

'Thank you, sir,' Josie said shyly, 'but it can only be the man who forced himself on me. That man over there.' Josie pointed to Dexter and Lawrence was regretting asking the question.

Judge Spellinger removed the large

gold pocket watch from his waistcoat, checked the time, frowned and then asked Lawrence if he was about finished with his questioning. He reminded Lawrence that the hot court-room was no place for someone in Josie's condition.

The judge gave a weary sigh and said, 'Thank you,' after Lawrence had said that he had no further questions.

Bilson asked Josie a few questions in an attempt to nullify the accusations made by Lawrence against her charac-ter, but she didn't help herself with some of her replies and he was afraid that the jury wouldn't see her as a sweet innocent girl.

Following a short recess, Dexter Hankin was called to the stand. He smiled in the direction of his sister, but he was showing none of his usual outward confidence. He pleaded not guilty to the charge and seemed calm under questioning from Bilson. He admitted being in Claymore around the time of the rape, but couldn't be sure of the exact date. He was absolutely certain that he had never met Josie Webster.

Bilson ignored Dexter's claim that he'd never met Josie and asked him if the meeting had taken place near the river. Dexter smiled and replied, 'No offence, but the young lady is not the sort of woman that I'm attracted to. She's too young and innocent-looking. I prefer the more experienced woman who knows what a man wants and enjoys it herself.' The comment caused his defence lawyer to frown. Lawrence had briefed Dexter not to volunteer any opinions and keep his answers simple. Now the jury would be thinking that Dexter Hankin was a pleasure seeker and not the hard-working son of a recently departed, highly respected rancher. Under Bilson's questioning, Dexter was talking himself into further trouble until he glanced over at Lawrence who made a gesture with his hand across his mouth to signal to his client to stop talking so much.

Lawrence took the unusual step of not questioning Dexter, having decided it might do more harm than good. Things had been going well until Hankin's big mouth and arrogance had placed him in danger of facing a noose around his neck. But Lawrence had an idea that might just save his client and he asked the judge if he could approach the bench.

Judge Spellinger was beginning to feel tired by the proceedings that had gone on much longer than he'd expected and he gave a weary sigh before answering.

'Very well, but if you are going to ask for an adjournment then you are going to need a very good reason. You have already taken up too much time with your irrelevant questions.'

Those gathered in the court looked on as Lawrence approached the bench and began talking to the judge who sat listening intently and then appeared thoughtful before he gave his response.

Judge Spellinger cleared his throat

and then addressed the jury.

'Defence counsel has made an unusual request which I have agreed to in order to give the defendant every opportunity to prove his innocence. I am going to call a short adjournment of fifteen minutes during which the court will be cleared. When the court resumes Miss Webster will be recalled to the witness stand. This court is adjourned for fifteen minutes.'

'The court will rise and reconvene in fifteen minutes.' boomed out the clerk of the court.

Josie looked pale and anxious when she returned to the noisy courtroom and flinched when Judge Spellinger banged the gavel on the desk and demanded silence. Josie took the stand again and when her eyes drifted towards the jury she saw the reason for the commotion that had erupted when the court had resumed. She was filled with anguish when the judge asked her to look at the two men sitting in front of the jury and identify which one of them attacked her. Dexter and Ben were sat upright, their faces solemn, as directed earlier by Lawrence. They wore identical, pale-blue shirts, pants and boots. Their black Stetsons were angled so that their faces were in clear view.

Robert Lawrence was usually calculating and analytical, but now he was gambling, and the stake was Dexter Hankin's life. He noted Josie's discomfort and uncertainty. He wanted to hear her say, 'I'm not sure.' That would do because then he could tell the jury she was unreliable. He wondered how many people in the court could tell the men apart, because he could. There was a resemblance, but it wasn't as though they looked like brothers, at least not to him.

'Take your time, Miss Webster,' said Judge Spellinger in a quiet sympathetic voice and then added 'Just point in the direction of the man and he will then stand up.'

The courtroom was spellbound as she raised her right hand. Lawrence's calmness had deserted him as he held his breath, realizing that his reputation would be in ruins if this stunt went wrong.

Some of those gathered had muttered their own guess as to who it was before Judge Spellinger directed the man standing up to identify himself to the court.

'My name is Ben Oakes.'

The courtroom erupted with various levels of groaning. Some of the women added their own comments about Josie and none was complimentary. Bilson looked dejected and Lawrence's face was impassive. Some men would have punched the air with a victory salute, but he was too professional to do that.

It took many thumps on the desk with the judge's gavel before the courtroom was once again in silence. Judge Spellinger announced that he was stopping the case. He expressed his sympathy for Josie Webster, but made it clear that neither Dexter Hankin nor Ben Oakes should ever be charged with the rape of the unfortunate woman.

Dexter couldn't contain his relief as he pumped Lawrence's hand and bestowed lavish praise on him before turning to hug his sister and then Wendel Collyer. In the midst of the celebration Wendel Collyer looked embarrassed and Ben slipped away from the courtroom and headed for the saloon. He'd wanted to see Madeline again, but she'd lowered her eyes when he'd looked at her. Perhaps she was thinking about the things that had been said about his past, including those he'd admitted to. Madeline would never have thought that he could have killed a single man, let alone four. She would be thinking that she didn't know him at all.

15

Shacker Moke had ridden the three miles from Claymore to his log cabin that nestled in the woods near the River Torrey. He had mixed feelings when he saw Caleb Webster's horse tied to the hitch rail. He didn't know how Caleb would take the news he was about to deliver. They'd been friends since they were boys, but Caleb had a mean streak and was likely to turn on anyone, especially when he'd been drinking hard liquor.

Shacker Moke was forty-two years old. He had a beer belly and it wouldn't be long before folks would say that he was almost as wide as he was tall which was only five foot four inches when he was at full stretch. One of his eyes was almost closed and wasn't much good for seeing out of since his pistol had backfired and a piece of metal had embedded itself in his eye. The bushy beard was the colour of a skunk with its odd mixture of black and white.

'Get in here, quick,' ordered Webster, before Moke had dismounted.

'I got you some more liquor,' said Moke, as he carried the two bottles inside.

'Never mind the liquor. What happened at the trial? I know it was today because some feller told me as I was riding in here.'

'It ain't good news, Caleb.'

'Just tell me what happened?'

Moke studied his friend before he replied. He hadn't seen a man change so much in just three weeks. The face was gaunt and the skin was deathly white. The grey eyes seemed staring and wild. Either Caleb had borrowed some big feller's shirt, or he'd lost one hell of a lot of weight.

'Have you gone deaf?' shouted Caleb. 'I asked you to tell me what happened at the trial.'

'The slippery son of a bitch,' said Webster, after Moke had told him that

Dexter Hankin had been cleared of Josie's rape. He pulled the cork from the whiskey bottle with his teeth and had gulped back nearly a third of its contents before he paused. 'You said Hankin, but the feller who did, you know what, to sweet Josie went by the name of Ben Oakes.'

'It's all a bit confusing, Caleb. Josie picked out this feller Hankin and then she picked out the other one, Ben Oakes, in the court. The judge dismissed the case and said neither of them could be charged in the future.'

'So it wasn't a lily-livered jury let my Josie down, but some dopey old judge who should be kicking up the daisies instead of making important decisions. There ain't no justice. That's why I wanted to take care of it myself.'

'Where have you been all these past weeks, Caleb? The marshal's been looking for you and Josie's been really worried. I think she thought you abandoned her because of the shame of her expecting a rapist's baby.'

'I went to sort things out for my Josie, but it didn't go like I hoped. I'll explain what happened later. So tell me more about what happened in court.'

Moke waited for Caleb to finish gulping the whiskey straight from the bottle before he spoke again. 'That city lawyer feller who defended Hankin was damned good, Caleb. He twisted everything and said that Josie was . . . ' Moke paused as he struggled to remember the word, but gave up. 'I forget what the big word was, but I think it meant that Josie was confused after what happened to her. He said that Dexter Hankin had lost his brother because someone had probably mistaken him for someone else. He told her not to make the same mistake and condemn an innocent man to an early grave.'

Caleb took another gulp of whiskey before he said, 'Maybe that feller who got killed, you know, the brother, was the real villain and got what he deserved.'

'It sure is confusing, Caleb. They said the Hankin brothers were alike and it was amazing seeing him and that other feller in court today because they looked alike as well.'

'So it looks as though Josie was confused and the feller that' — Webster struggled with the thought of what had happened to Josie and then continued — 'did that vile thing to Josie must have been Oakes after all. So did the marshal arrest him after the trial?'

Moke looked uncomfortable and said that he'd already explained that the judge had said that neither Oakes, nor Hankin could be brought to trial again.

'Well, we don't need any trial. We're going into town and finish this off,' said Webster as he staggered to his feet. 'But first I need to know how Josie took the news.'

'She'd already left the court before the verdict was reached, but she did look pretty upset when they were questioning her. That lawyer feller said some cruel things. He said that she was full of liquor at the time it happened. He accused her of lying to protect someone else, or wanting to have a bit of fun and afterwards had got worried sick in case she ended up with a swollen belly. Well, he didn't exactly say a swollen belly, but that's what he meant. You know, a momma.'

Caleb became real agitated, 'What did he mean 'protecting someone else'? The girl has never ever had a boyfriend, at least none that I knew of.'

Moke took another swig from the whiskey bottle and then cleared his throat. 'There's something you ought to know, Caleb. Some folks have been saying that you and Josie living under the same roof and sometimes sharing a bed weren't natural.'

Caleb's face reddened and he slammed down the whiskey bottle.

'What evil, gossiping bastards suggested such a thing? She's my kinfolk and there ain't anything wrong with us living together. There are things that not even you know about me and Josie.'

'I remember her ma Mary. She was a real pretty woman. It was a damn shame she and your brother Henry died when they were both so young.'

'You best tell me who those evil-minded shits are, Moke, because I intend to teach them a lesson.'

'I don't know who they are, Caleb. It was just tittle-tattle and ain't worth getting yourself locked up for.'

'I'll find out who they are and when I do I'll make them wish they'd kept their nasty thoughts to themselves. Anyhow, I need to concentrate on the feller who did that to my Josie before he leaves town and I need you to do something for me.'

Moke looked uncomfortable and said, 'You know I ain't much good when it comes to fightin', Caleb.'

'I don't want you to do any fighting. I just want you to ride over to my place and look after Josie if she turns up.'

'Don't you worry, Caleb, I'll make sure she's all right. Now you be careful,' Moke cautioned, relieved that he wasn't going to be involved in whatever Caleb got up to in town. The two friends downed the remaining whiskey from their bottles before riding off together, but not before Caleb revealed to his friend that he was Josie's pa and not her uncle.

16

Josie Webster was seated in the shade on a bench outside the general store when the street was filled with people who had streamed from the white wooden courthouse. She'd hurried from the court after identifying Ben Oakes. When she saw the two men talking outside the saloon she knew what the verdict had been. They were still wearing identical clothes and they really did look alike. She had been certain that Dexter Hankin was her attacker, and now she was confused and frightened. She might have been the cause of an innocent man being hanged. Her attacker had seemed so nice that evening when he'd ridden by as she was picking flowers near the river. Some of those folks in court had given her disapproving looks, mostly the women, including those she'd known all her life and always been friendly towards her until now. It would have been different if Uncle Caleb hadn't abandoned her as well. She had brought shame on him and perhaps it was best that he hadn't heard that legal man say all those cruel things about her. She was a churchgoing girl, but he'd made her sound like a common saloon girl. She wouldn't be able to go to church any more, knowing that her face would burn with shame whenever the Reverend Vance preached about the sinful daughters and their fornicating. She didn't know the meaning of fornicating, but it didn't sound like something that nice girls would do.

Josie slumped back in the seat as two ladies passed by. They looked in her direction, just for a moment, before averting their eyes and hurrying past. Josie saw both of them look back and she had no doubt that they were talking about her. She reached down and lifted the small bag that she'd placed between her feet and took out the apple which was nestled next to the small pistol. Uncle Caleb had taught her how to shoot and insisted that she always carried it in her bag. He'd been so protective towards her and she knew that he felt he'd failed her just this once. Perhaps it was his guilt that had forced him to leave her, rather than the shame. He said he was going to sort out some business over at her Aunt Lillian's and would be back in a few days, but that was over three weeks ago.

Josie had never known her own pa, who was Uncle Caleb's brother and had been killed by a poisonous snake when she was just a baby. She had no memories of her ma, who had died from some mysterious disease and Josie had never really missed her until now. Josie had rested her head on the back of the seat and was on the point of drifting off to sleep when she was startled by the voice.

'Are you all right?'

It took a moment for Josie to focus

on the person who was concerned about her.

'I'm fine, just a bit sleepy. It's been a long day for me.'

'I'm Madeline Hankin.'

'I saw you in court,' Josie said. 'I was just taking a rest before I go home.'

There was awkwardness between them and Madeline sensed Josie's discomfort and said, 'As long as you are all right. I'll be leaving with my brother in a short while if the train is on time. I hope everything goes well for you and your baby.'

Josie didn't say anything and Madeline said goodbye and walked back towards the hotel.

* * *

Madeline's travel bag had been brought down to the hotel lobby and she took a seat near the door. She had arranged to meet Dexter and Wendel Collyer there so that they could travel to the railroad station together, but she was restless.

She was regretting that she had agreed with her brother that she wouldn't speak to Ben before she left, but she wanted to make sure that he knew that he would still be welcome at the ranch. She was confused about some of the things that Ben had admitted to in court, especially about having killed those men. There was still no explanation as to why Josie's attacker had used the name Ben Oakes, or why Ben had denied ever being in Claymore before. Ben had a side to him that she'd never known.

Dexter joined his sister at the table in the hotel foyer and was about to order some drinks when Madeline asked him to go and find Ben. Dexter frowned and said, 'I thought we agreed it was best not to see him again.'

'I don't, not today, but I want you to tell him that he'll be welcome if he returns to the ranch and that he can work for us.'

Dexter asked his sister if she was sure that's what she wanted, and when she made it clear that it was, he promised to find Ben. He would keep his promise, but he would tell Ben that Madeline never wanted to see him again and that she was now convinced that he'd killed Todd.

★　★　★

Josie was about to get up from the bench outside the store when she saw Dexter Hankin and Ben Oakes make their way up Main Street heading for the livery. She decided she would wait and watch to see if they left town. Perhaps once they were gone she could get on with her life or whatever was left of it. She'd spotted Deputy Tuke earlier and wondered if he would ever have plucked up the courage to ask her to go courting. She knew he'd come close to asking her out a few times and Uncle Caleb had teased her about having a lawman in the family one day. Lenny Tuke wasn't exactly a handsome man, but she liked him despite his funny habit of sniffing. She'd thought it was just a cold at first, but decided it was some kind of nervous affliction. Anyway, he'd hardly said a word to her when he'd ridden her back home from the marshal's office after she'd identified Dexter Hankin. She wasn't sweet Josie any more. She was soiled and even if Tuke still liked her, his ma would make sure that he kept away from her.

She reached down and lifted the red coloured cloth that was on top of the basket and looked again at the small handgun. Uncle Caleb said it may not be very lady-like carrying a gun, but she might need it one day when he wasn't around if anyone came snooping near their remote cabin. She'd planned to use it on Dexter Hankin as soon as she set eyes on him in court, but she'd lost her nerve. She would be shooting the father of her unborn child, but she remembered how her attacker had just grinned and left her weeping as he had ridden off. She stood up when she saw the rider coming out of the livery. Well, at least one of them was leaving town. As the rider came level with the store she reached into her bag and pulled out the pistol, stepped off the sidewalk and fired two shots at the man she now knew for certain was her rapist. The first bullet hit him in the shoulder and the second in the chest as he fell with a thud into the dusty street when the horse reared. His face was already ashen and she was certain that he was dead as he lay still. The distinctive grey horse had galloped away after being spooked by the gunfire, but had returned and stood calmly beside its fallen rider.

17

Caleb Webster pulled his mount to a halt outside the Derby Saloon and rushed up the wooden steps to the sidewalk without bothering to tie the reins to the hitch rail. Moke had told him that he'd seen Hankin and Oakes near the saloon when he was riding out of town. Caleb could never live with himself unless he got justice for his Josie. The law had failed her, but he wouldn't. He'd put an end to this right now.

There were some startled faces when they turned to see who had burst through the saloon doors and roared out, 'Where is he?' and then added, 'Where's the feller who violated my sweet Josie and fooled the dopey old judge? Show yourself, you spineless good for nothing.' Caleb scanned the saloon, hoping that the man he hated so much would identify himself, or some-one would point him out.

'Come on, you yeller belly,' he roared again, with a wild look in his eyes.

'He's not here, Caleb. He's over at Doc Morrison's,' said the barman.

For a moment Caleb was puzzled until someone said, 'Josie shot him. Why don't you go and find her?'

'But he's still alive though?' asked Webster, directing his enquiry at the barman, but someone else answered.

'Not for long judging by the look of him as they carried him to the doc's surgery,' said Silas Gilks who worked as a printer at the local newspaper.

'Did you see Josie shoot him?' Caleb asked.

'I sure did. I was almost within touching distance. She's one hell of a shot, that girl. She hit him twice as he rode past her and she said something about it being the rapist's horse. It was a grey with a strange black pattern on its flanks and I don't reckon there could be another like it in the whole of

Arizona. Josie threw her gun into the street and just ran off.'

'You'd better not be bullshitting me because if you are I'll be back and you'll all be sorry,' said Caleb, and turned and headed for the door while pulling his pistol from its holster.

'He ain't worth hanging for, Caleb,' shouted the barman, but Caleb didn't hear him and was soon heading down the sidewalk to the doc's surgery located just beyond the general store and close to where Josie had used the skill that he'd taught her.

Doc Morrison had been dozing in his chair when he heard the banging on his door. He rose from the chair and glanced down at the surgery bed as he made his way to attend to his frantic caller. Whoever wanted his services sounded desperate.

Doc Morrison had barely opened the door when a wild eyed Caleb Webster pushed him aside. 'Where's the feller who should be facing a hanging for what he did to my Josie?'

'If you mean Dexter Hankin, I guess he's back in Tremaine Creek. He left here by train this afternoon with his sister.'

Webster looked puzzled. 'Then who did my Josie shoot? Is that him lying there?'

'He's the man that Josie shot. His name is Ben Oakes, but if you've come to finish him off then you're too late because he's already dead.'

Caleb glowered at Ben's ghostly face. 'So Josie must have realized that he was the one.' He raised his pistol above his head preparing to smash it into Ben's face.

Caleb had left the door open when he'd burst into the surgery and he hadn't heard the footsteps on the sidewalk.

'Drop the gun, Caleb.' It was Marshal Slaney and he'd just cocked the pistol he was pointing at Caleb's back.

Caleb froze and lowered his gun, but still kept his eyes fixed on Ben.

'Is Oakes dead?' asked the marshal.

'He was hanging in there for awhile, but he never had much of a chance,' replied the doc.

'Step away from the bed, Caleb. We need to find Josie. She ran away after the shooting and we ain't been able to find her. Perhaps you might know where she would go to hide.'

Caleb followed the marshal's order and the tension lifted, but he was soon back in threatening mood when he said, 'You'd better not bury him in the town cemetery. He doesn't deserve to lie near decent folks.'

'Let's go, Caleb. It'll be dark soon and Josie will be out there and frightened as hell. We need to find her soon, because I reckon we're in for another cold night.'

The marshal and Webster had just stepped into Main Street when Ben gave a low groan. 'Shush,' whispered Doc Morrison, 'or my lies and acting will be for nothing. I'd always fancied going on stage and becoming an actor and after that performance I think I might have made it.'

The doc had managed to wink at the marshal when he'd said that Ben was dead. But the doc was thinking that his lie would be a truth in a few hours' time unless a miracle happened and then he wouldn't have to worry about Caleb finding out.

18

It was just four days after Josie had shot, and almost killed him, when Ben defied Doc Morrison's advice and prepared to leave Claymore. Ben had been disappointed when Dexter had told him Madeline now believed he'd killed Todd and she didn't want to see him again. After the trial Ben and Dexter had gone to the livery to make arrangements for Ben to pick up the Hankin horse on which Dexter had ridden into town. Dexter had given it to Ben for helping him when he'd sent the telegraph to his pa to arrange legal help.

Ben had been saddened to hear that Josie Webster's body had been found floating in the river the day after she'd shot him. It seems that Caleb Webster had made all kinds of threats and promises at her graveside and revealed that he was actually Josie's pa and not her uncle. He'd kept it a secret from her, but had planned to tell when she was seventeen years old which would have been six months from now. Webster had disappeared again after the funeral and not even his friend Moke knew where he had gone.

Ben had decided to leave Claymore when he'd spoken to Marshal Slaney and, according to the marshal, there was an explanation for Caleb Webster's previous absence. He had gone to his sister's to make arrangements for Josie to move in with her and while he was there he'd developed some sort of fever. At the time of Todd's killing, Caleb Webster was close to dying himself, or at least that's what he'd told the marshal.

Doc Morrison was having his usual mid-morning doze in his chair when Ben called and told him that he was riding out and had called to thank him for saving his life, despite Josie and Caleb Webster's determination to end it.

'Now you take care of yourself, boy. I don't want my good work going to waste,' said Doc Morrison, as he shook Ben's hand.

'I will, Doc. I owe you a lot and I don't just mean healing these wounds. I might have thought I was going crazy if you hadn't explained about my head injuries.'

When Doc Morrison had attended to Ben's recent wounds he'd recognized him as the cowboy whom he had treated months earlier for a wound on the back of his head. Ben couldn't even remember his name at the time and he'd left the doc's care before he'd fully recovered. The doc told Ben that was the reason he had some gaps in his memory and couldn't recall ever being to Claymore Ridge before.

'Will I ever get my memory back, Doc?' Ben asked, even though he might remember something that he'd rather not.

'The brain is a complex thing, son, and we don't know a lot about it. I wouldn't worry too much. It's not as though you can't remember new things. You just have a small gap in your life. I know lots of men who can't remember things that their wives tell them a few minutes earlier, especially if it means helping with the chores.'

They both laughed and Ben moved towards the door and then stepped out into the street. Ben was walking towards his horse when Doc Morrison shook his head and said, 'That man's a walking miracle. I've never known a man lose so much blood and not die.'

Ben led his horse to the marshal's office and tied its reins to the hitch rail. He entered the office, hoping the marshal was in because he wanted to thank him as well before he headed off.

'I thought you'd still be recovering at the doc's,' said the marshal, and invited Ben to take a seat. Ben told him that he was feeling much better and he was leaving town after their chinwag.

'Will you head for the Hankin place, now that your name's been cleared?'

'I won't be welcome there, but I need to tell them that Caleb Webster wasn't Todd's killer and they will be left wondering again. If only I could have got a closer look at the killer instead of seeing his back disappearing into the distance.'

'It's a pity that Mexican girl couldn't describe him either. Maybe Josie's rapist and the Hankin boy's killer will never be found.' The marshal paused before he added, 'I took a look at that grey horse of yours the other day and it certainly is unusual. Surely if that horse belonged to Todd Hankin then he's got to be the rapist.'

Ben defended Todd, but it sure looked like the marshal's deduction was right because Josie had remembered the horse.

The marshal didn't comment on Ben's rejection of the idea that Todd had been Josie's attacker and looked solemn when he said, 'It was a damned shame that lovely young girl ending up floating in a river,' and then added, 'a tragic waste of a young life and she was a lovely looking girl as well.'

Deputy Tuke had been standing near the rifle rack looking sullen and he glowered at Ben with hate-filled eyes as he headed towards the door, but he had a farewell message for Ben. 'I hope you burn in hell, Oakes.'

Ben was taken back by the ferocity of the comment.

'Don't mind him. He's taken Josie's death really bad. He was sweet on the girl and probably would have ended up marrying her had she not . . . ' Marshal Slaney didn't finish his words and Ben asked him if perhaps Tuke might have been Todd's killer.

'Now hold on there, feller. You're linking the killing with the rape and forgetting that Josie couldn't remember the name of the town near the ranch where the rapist said he worked. So, Tuke or no one else from here would have known where to find him. I should have thought of that before I suggested it might have been poor Caleb Webster.'

'I suppose you're right, Marshal, except that I could have mentioned it to someone. But in case you're wondering about this business of Josie and Todd's horse I can tell you that Todd was no rapist.'

'From what you told the court there might be some folks out there who might want to settle an old score with you and it was you that the killer was looking for.'

'That thought has haunted me ever since the day Todd was killed,' said Ben.

'By the way, have you seen Dexter Hankin?' asked the marshal.

Ben was puzzled by the question and reminded the marshal that Dexter had left town with his sister.

'I wish he had,' replied the marshal with a sigh. 'The man's a damned nuisance. I had to tell him to leave the saloon the other night. He was as drunk as a skunk and pestering one of the girls.'

'I wonder why he didn't leave?' asked a puzzled Ben.

'On the day of the trial and shortly after you'd been shot I told Tuke to escort the Hankins to the railroad station. Tuke waited for the train to leave and saw Dexter arguing with his sister and the lawyer who had accompanied her. Dexter stormed off and definitely didn't leave town. I forgot to mention that Madeline Hankin was real upset when she heard about you being shot. She wanted to stay and see if you were all right, but her brother told her that they would miss their train and you were going to die anyway. Maybe that's what they were arguing about at the station.'

Ben was thinking that Marshal Slaney was one hell of a lawman the way he figured things out. He shook the marshal's hand, thanked him once again for his help and stepped out onto Main Street, just in time to see Tuke riding off in the direction that Ben planned to take.

Ben pulled up the grey on the outskirts of town and took a long look down Main Street. He had a feeling that he wouldn't be returning.

The grey was just as he imagined and had a turn of speed like no other horse he'd ever ridden. He'd pushed her at full gallop until he reached the start of the hills not far out of town. He felt good. He sensed that he would be ready for a new start once he had delivered the news to Madeline about Todd's killer not being Caleb Webster.

He had no fear of riding the trail on which he could easily have died on his way to Claymore, because this time he was well stocked with food and water. He was reliving some of the horrors of the journey to Claymore when the sound of two shots fired in quick succession spooked the grey. Ben was thrown from his saddle and hit the ground with a thud, causing him to cry out in pain as he landed on his shoulder. He didn't need to look to know that the wound had opened and his shirt was wet with blood. The grey scampered off and Ben scrambled for cover behind some boulders as two more shots were fired. Whoever the son of a bitch was, he was either some distance away, or not a very good shot. Ben didn't know why, but he suddenly thought of cross-eyed Billy Cobb, the Hankin stable lad and not Tuke.

'You're a dead man, Oakes,' the voice called out, but Ben was unable to identify the caller.

The voice didn't sound like Tuke's, but Ben couldn't be certain.

'I never figured you for a sly shooter, Tuke. Why don't you come out and show yourself. Be a man that Josie Webster would have been proud to marry.'

The response was two more shots that hit the rock that Ben was sheltering behind. Ben was hoping that his remarks would anger Tuke and it seemed that they had. Maybe it would force him into making a move. Ben dragged himself to the next rock and his assailant seized his chance and fired. Ben's agonizing scream echoed around the rocks before he stopped and started groaning. His attacker waited until there was complete silence before he began moving forward. He smiled when he saw the rocks smeared with the blood of the man who he'd grown to hate. Now he could make plans, or so he thought, until Ben ordered him to drop his gun. He'd intended to obey the instruction, but made the mistake of turning in the direction of Ben's voice. Ben's single shot hit the man in the chest causing him to drop his gun as he stumbled against the rock. If Ben had been a gambling man he would have had difficulty betting on the identity of the man who wanted him dead. Lenny Tuke had been his favourite, or had Caleb Webster returned, hell bent on some misguided revenge? Ben had remembered how poor a shot Dexter Hankin had been. Todd had once said that Dexter couldn't hit a barn door from twenty yards.

'I thought you were dead, you son of a bitch,' the man gasped, as Ben stood over him. The face was familiar, but it wasn't Dexter Hankin.

'You didn't even hit me,' replied Ben, 'This blood is from an old wound and the girl that did this was a better shot than you.'

'You'd be dead now, if that damned rifle hadn't gone all funny on me.'

'Why, Macey? I suppose all this is about Madeline. She would never have married you, knowing that her pa never really liked you.'

'She would have, because old Milton would have been beholden to me for killing you. And with you and Todd out of the way he would have needed someone to take over the ranch.'

'You killed Todd, didn't you?' Ben asked.

'He warned me off trying to see Madeline and threatened to turn me in because of what I did to that girl Josie when we three came to Claymore. He should have kept his nose out of my business.' Macey paused and his face was twisted in pain until he managed a sly smile and said, 'The plan almost worked when you got the blame, but that was just luck. I thought I'd got rid of you when someone left you for dead in Claymore.'

Macey's eyes were half closed now as though he was about to drift off to sleep.

'So it was you who attacked that poor girl?' Ben said, but he couldn't recall Todd mentioning that Macey was with them in Claymore.

'That stupid girl fell for my sweet talking and then went all frigid on . . . '

Macey's eyes closed and his breathing was laboured.

Ben offered to help him, but he could see by the amount of blood pumping from his chest that he was beyond help. Macey gave a low groan and never spoke again. He mustn't have heard the news that Milton Hankin was dead.

Ben was tempted to bury Macey in a shallow grave, turn his horse lose and ride on, but decided that he would return his body to Claymore and tell the marshal that poor Josie had been wrong all along, but at least her attacker was now dead. Ben used the water from his canteen to clean his opened wound, but it was soon oozing blood after he'd struggled to lay Macey's body across the killer's horse ready for his return to Claymore.

★ ★ ★

A small crowd gathered round when Ben dismounted outside the marshal's office. He ignored their enquiries and gingerly mounted the steps, weakened by his fall and the loss of blood. He would be calling on Doc Morrison later, but he needed to report in to Marshal Slaney first.

'Jesus, boy, what happened to you?' asked the marshal, and then ordered Tuke to get Ben a seat.

Tuke offered Ben the seat, but there was a look of satisfaction on his face because of Ben's obvious pain.

'I've got a dead man outside. He

tried to ambush me and I ended up shooting him.'

'Doc Morrison is going to be busy again. He's already had one customer this morning, but he couldn't help him. This is going to come as a shock to you because it was Dexter Hankin. You hadn't left town more than a few minutes when a feller came in and reported there was a body in an alley near the Salt Box saloon. By the colour and texture of his skin I reckoned it happened last night. He'd been shot in the back of his head.'

Ben took a while for it to sink in and then was thinking that Madeline was in for more bad news and that maybe someone had put a curse on the Hankin family.

When Ben had finished telling the marshal about Macey admitting to killing Todd Hankin, and raping Josie, Tuke smirked and said, 'He sure managed to say a lot for a man who was dying.'

Ben was tempted to ignore Tuke, but

replied, 'I think he said it to sort of gloat and he didn't seem in any discomfort at first. I guess he just bled to death.'

The marshal was looking thoughtful and Ben asked if something was bothering him.

'A couple of things, I suppose. I know you told me that you must have been in Claymore with Todd Hankin, but had no recollection because of that blow you took to the head, but you never mentioned this feller Macey being here. The other thing is this business about Josie shooting you because you were riding that distinctive grey horse.'

Ben had been puzzled about Macey being in Claymore as well, but only because Todd hadn't mentioned him being with them. But as for the horse, he remembered Macey always wanting to ride it, just like he had. Ben explained once again about his memory loss and gave the explanation that Macey sometimes rode Todd's horse.

'I still think it's odd,' grumbled Tuke,

'And I think it's time you did your rounds instead of sulking,' said the marshal.

Tuke gave Ben a final glower, picked up his hat and headed out into the street.

The marshal shook his head and said, 'That feller is more trouble than he's worth. You don't fancy hanging around here and becoming a deputy, do you? I could do with someone who can handle himself.'

'No thanks, Marshal, but I might take up your offer if things don't work out in Tremaine Creek, or should I say, the Hankin Ranch. I plan to head there tomorrow, after Dexter's been buried. I won't be attending that son of a bitch Macey's funeral, but I expect you'll want his full name and whatever other details I can give you.'

Before Ben left he asked the marshal if Dexter Hankin had left anything that his sister might want as a keepsake, but the marshal said he had no valuables on him and even his gun was missing.

Ben headed for the doc's surgery and was surprised at the welcome he got. 'Well if it isn't my best customer,' said the doc with a shake of the head.

Ben apologized for messing up the doc's good work and the doc told him that he would miss Ben when he finally left town because he had a feeling that things were going to get pretty quiet.

Doc Morrison applied a new dressing to Ben's wound and offered him the use of a bed in the back room of the surgery. He'd told him that he occasionally used it to lay out a deceased person until the undertaker took them away. Ben was too tired and weak to worry about such things and gratefully accepted the doc's hospitality.

Dexter Hankin's funeral was a simple affair, but the minister had said some kind words from the information that Ben had supplied and at least his grave was marked and well away from where Macey had been buried in an unmarked one. Maybe Madeline would visit her brother's grave one day. As soon as the funeral was over Ben rode out of Claymore on the distinctive grey and black horse that Todd had ridden into Claymore all those months earlier.

When Ben reached the spot where Macey had fired at him, he pulled on the reins, bringing Speckly to a halt and then dismounted. Something had been preying on his mind and he knew he would curse himself if he didn't check it out. He scanned the area and tried to locate the exact spot where he had been when he had fooled Macey into thinking he was dead. When he saw the dried blood on the rocks he knew he was in the right place. He didn't have to search for long before he spotted the pistol that Macey had been brandishing when he'd come to check that Ben was dead. Ben picked up the distinctive pearl-handled Colt .44 that had belonged to Dexter Hankin. Ben had no doubt that it was the one that had been stolen from Dexter's body by his killer. Ben placed the pistol in one of the saddle-bags and gingerly mounted the grey. Ewen Macey must have been evil to be prepared to kill the way he had to just to further his own gain.

Madeline Hankin was going to be in for a surprise when she saw him because, according to Marshal Slaney, she thought Ben was probably dead. Ben was puzzled why she had been so concerned about him when she had discovered that he'd been shot by Josie, if she believed that he had killed Todd. He didn't expect to be made welcome, but just hoped that she would believe what he had to tell her. She had a right to know that Ewen Macey had killed Todd, and she needed to know that Dexter would never be returning home because he had died by the same hand that killed Todd.

Wendel Collyer had confided in Ben that Milton Hankin had been involved in a long-standing affair with a former saloon girl, and made regular payments to her after their son was born. He'd threatened to stop the payments if she ever told anyone about their affair. The woman had died some years ago.

By the time Ben reached the Hankin ranch and met Madeline again he would have decided whether to tell her that he had killed her half-brother, Ewen Macey.

19

Ben waved to his buddies and turned his horse in the direction of the nearby Hankin ranch. The cowhands had called him Boss when they shouted their farewells to him and that still made him feel embarrassed. He had just returned from his third visit to Claymore Ridge since he'd killed Ewen Macey there nearly three years ago. He'd been married to Madeline Hankin for almost two years and they had a beautiful daughter, called Sandy, named after the late Grandma Sandy, which is how Ben now referred to the saloon girl who had brought him up.

Ben was looking forward to the welcome he would get from Madeline. It would be just like the unexpected one she'd given him when he'd gone to tell her the news about Dexter's death and his showdown with Ewen Macey. He'd put two and two together and figured that Dexter had lied to him when he'd delivered the message that Madeline blamed him for Todd's death. But he didn't tell Madeline about the lies, fearing that it would spoil her memories of Dexter. And he didn't tell her that Ewen Macey was her half-brother. Ben had spoken to Wendel Collyer, the family lawyer, and they had agreed that telling her would serve no purpose and might tarnish Madeline's image of her late father whom she had worshipped.

Claymore Ridge wasn't exactly cattle country, but Milton Hankin had always bought breeding stock from a small ranch close to the town and that had been the reason for Ben revisiting the place from time to time. It was during his first return to the town where he had nearly died that Marshal Slaney had told him a few interesting things. Caleb Webster had been killed by his old friend Shacker Moke. Shacker had struck Caleb from behind with a small log after Caleb had demanded money from him to buy liquor. Caleb had been told about Macey being Josie's rapist, but he never recovered from Josie's death and would have drunk himself to death sooner or later. Ben had smiled when he'd heard that Deputy Lenny Tuke had become a barman and married one of the saloon girls even though his ma had threatened never to speak to him if he did.

Ben urged Speckly forward when he saw Madeline waving to him as she stood outside the ranch house. There were still gaps in his memory about his first visit to Claymore Ridge and some memories he would never forget, but wished he could.

Grandma Sandy had been right about luck following him. He hadn't fired his gun in anger since he'd killed Macey and there was no mistaking that he had found contentment.